Ms. Nice Nasty 2

ISBN: 1519739648

ISBN-13: 978-1519739643

Dedication

This book, like all the rest, is dedicated to YOU; those of you who continue to believe in me, book after book! Please don't stop. Your support and encouragement is the fuel I need to keep writing!

My Thanks

As always, I must thank God for entrusting me with such an amazing gift. Every day I am grateful He doesn't limit my gift of writing, He simply allows me to write so writing is what I shall do.

I will not go into details and try to name everybody this time around but to my husband, Willie, my children Gabrielle and Christopher and my entire family; know that I love each of you for supporting me.

A special thanks to Laquisha, Kena and Unique for being my Beta Readers; to Aija Butler (AMB Designs) for my cover design and Stephanie for editing. You chicks rock!

To every one of you, who support Lakisha, THANK YOU!!! I cannot believe this is the final book in my second series. How awesome is that? I would not be the author I am without readers like you. It is because of you, purchasing and downloading my books and then recommending and reviewing them, that pushes me to be greater the next time. Don't ever stop.

To each of you who are on this journey, don't ever allow the ink to run dry in your pen or the lead to break on your pencil, you can do this! The only obstacle in your way is … you!

Again, I thank you from the bottom of my heart!

Ms. Nice Nasty 2

Where we left off ...

"You ready for the party?" Thomas asks walking into the room.

"As ever as I could be. I just can't believe I am now officially a judge," I tell him standing up from my vanity.

"Wow."

"What?"

"You look amazing."

Yea, Sam did a fantastic job with the dress she sent me. It arrived a few days ago and I hadn't even bothered to try it on because I know Sam and she knows my body well. The black and silver long sheath evening gown is contoured to my body just right. It's off the shoulder and the back swings low enough to show skin but still maintain a level of class. I paired it with these black and silver Giuseppe Zanotti stilettos that fit it perfectly. *Yea, I know.* I don't normally spend that much on a pair of shoes but when I saw these, I had to have them.

"I guess you like the dress," I smile.

"Yes. Is it one of Lyn's?"

"No. It's from my friend Sam in Miami."

"Sam?" he asks looking confused.

"Yes. She sent it to me — it came the other day."

"Oh ok," he replies when he realizes Sam is a she and not a he.

"Is everybody ready and is the car here?"

"No, it should be here in ten minutes."

"Okay. I'm on my way down."

========

We make it to the Hilton where the party is being held. My mom is in charge, of course, so she's off handling last-minute things in the ballroom. My family is at the bar and the girls haven't arrived yet. We get there early because Thomas and I have decided to stay overnight, so we go to check in first. Thomas has made sure all our bags and everything are already put away but we still have time to wait. My mom has an entire program prepared and I can't step one foot into where the party is being held. She has a private area set up for me so Thomas and I are back there sitting and drinking wine.

"Dang, I forgot my earrings."

"Where are they? I'll get them," Thomas says, getting up.

"They're in the bag that's inside of my cosmetic bag inside of… You know what, never mind. I need to freshen up my makeup anyway. I'll be right back. Give me the room key."

"Okay, but don't be long. You know how your mom is. We are set to go into the party in thirty minutes."

"I know."

"Babe, thirty minutes."

"I'll be back in ten, promise."

I make it into the room and it is dark. *Dang, why didn't Thomas leave any lights on?* As soon as I reach for the light switch, someone starts clapping. "Well, bravo Judge Camille Shannon."

"Who's there?" I ask because I don't recognize her voice right off.

"They say you can't turn a hoe into a housewife but I guess you can turn a hoe into a judge, huh?"

"Who are you?" I ask again, this time getting angry.

"Even after everything I did to sabotage you, them motherfuckers still gave you the job and you accepted!"

"I guess you didn't do enough. Look, you may have time to stay here all night but I have a party to attend, so either show yourself and say what you have to say or get the fuck out my room."

"Who said anything about you getting back to the party?"

I start laughing.

"Something funny?" she asks.

"Yes, your sad ass. You've gone through a whole lot to screw me over, and for what? What have I done to you? Did I fuck your husband better than you could or did I suck your girlfriend's clit so good that she was calling my name at home? And now you've set out on a mission to destroy Camille Shannon. How's that working for you?"

"Fuck you!" she screams.

"Is that what you want?" I ask, moving close to her.

"Stop!"

"Or what? Isn't this what you want?" I ask moving closer to her, rubbing myself. "Wasn't all of this about you getting to me? Here I am boo."

"Now you want me?" she asks, softening.

I stop. "What do you mean, now?"

"Do you want me now, Cam?"

"Obviously I don't or we wouldn't both be here and you wouldn't be working so hard to ruin my life. So, tell me: what did I do or what didn't I do to deserve all this?"

"You don't know?"

"Girl, I don't have time for your games. Show yourself or let me get what I came for and you can stay here until I get back."

"Or I can go downstairs and ruin your party and your career."

"Go ahead."

She doesn't move so I walk towards the bathroom.

"Where are you going?"

"To get my earrings. You've wasted enough of my time with this foolishness."

I go into the bathroom and get my earrings and fix my lip gloss. This damn fool is still sitting or standing in the dark when I come out.

"So, what are you going to do? Are you coming to the party or you staying here?"

"You must think you are invincible."

"No, but I am tired. Tired of dealing with a coward who calls from a block number, who busts windows out of people's cars, who leaves notes on windows, who sends pictures and calls news stations. I'm tired and I'm fed up."

"Then why aren't you tired of playing with people's feelings?"

"Stop getting your fucking feelings involved and they won't get hurt."

"You are one cold bitch."

"No, my name is Cam; take me or leave me," I declare walking towards the door.

"Stop!" she yells.

"Or what?"

"Or I'll blow your brains out." She turns on the light to reveal a gun pointed directly at me.

I start laughing.

"Why are you laughing?" she asks.

"Because you are one crazy bitch but I never expected this from you. You did all this after getting your pussy ate a few times? Damn! I knew I was good, but damn!"

"Fuck you Cam! You think you can make people fall in love with you and then you can just walk all over them! Fuck you!"

"Girl, ain't nobody walked over you. You have a husband. You knew what this was before you opened your legs and invited my head in between them so go on with all that. You got caught up and you know it."

"Caught up?"

"Yes, you got caught up by Ms. Nice Nasty and you couldn't handle it so you tried to drag my name and career into it, but it backfired on your raggedy ass. And since that didn't work, you're going to kill me now?"

"I might."

"Go ahead, but with your track record, you'll miss," I laugh, knowing damn well I am scared as hell.

"You're so sure, huh?" She raises the gun as someone uses a key to open the door.

"Babe, your mom is— What the hell?" Thomas yells as a gunshot rings out!

Chapter 1

"What the fuck!" Thomas yells as the bullet passes his head and lodges into the door.

"You crazy bitch!" I scream, running towards Jyema.

"Stop before I shoot at your ass too."

"And then what, Jyema? What is your endgame?" When she doesn't answer, I continue. "You haven't thought that far, have you?" I laugh. "You stupid motherfucker! It's always you cute chicks that's crazy as fuck!"

"Camille, what in the hell is going on?"

"Yea, Camille, why don't you tell your husband what is going on?" Jyema laughs.

"I am so glad you find this funny but answer this: what has been your point in all of this? You've been stalking me for months, calling me all times of day and night, leaving notes and pictures, busting windows out of my car, calling my job and for what?"

"She's been the one doing all those things?" Thomas asks, pointing at Jyema. "I bet you were the one that blamed Chelle for all that stuff too?"

"Shut up!" she screams. "Shut the fuck up both of you! Thomas, she doesn't care about your whining ass, can't you see that? In fact, she doesn't care about anybody but herself."

"Girl," I laugh, "what is your point? Telling him is going to do what — make him leave me? Oh, I get it. You're mad because I wouldn't spend any more time with you."

"You pushed me off like I was nothing. Like I didn't mean shit to you."

"Do you hear yourself? We weren't in a relationship. We were two consenting adults enjoying each other's company, making each other feel good, but now your ass has gone crazy."

"I'm not crazy. I just wanted you and you blew me off!"

"You have a whole husband," I say to her.

"And? You do too, but it didn't stop you from coming to me."

"For fun, Jyema! For fucking fun, but now you're standing here on the night I am supposed to be celebrating my installation to judgeship with a gun pointed at me and my husband."

"Wow!" Thomas says. "Just when I think our lives can't get any worse. Isn't she Brock's wife?"

"Don't start, Thomas. Now is not the time."

"It's never the time. What else is it going to take for you to see you need help? Standing here with this crazy bit—"

"Say it and I'll put a bullet in your ass," Jyema warns walking over to Thomas.

"Okay, stop. Just calm down. What do you want?" I ask her.

"I want you to leave with me."

"What? And go where? To Happilyeverafterville? You do know that security is probably out in the hallway as we speak?"

"I don't know! Just shut up and move," she replies, opening the door.

"I'm not going anywhere with you."

"Yes, you are. Let's go." She grabs my arm.

"Look, fool, why don't you leave before the police get here in order to save both of us a lot of embarrassment."

"I'm not going anywhere without you."

"And she isn't getting out of here without going to jail," Thomas says.

"Drop the gun!" a police officer shouts.

She pushes me back into the room, closes the door and begins to panic.

"Jyema, look. You need to open the door and we'll figure this shit out. I am sure the media is all over this by now and this is the last thing I need."

"Fuck! It's always about you, Cam! I ought to shoot your ass right now and get it over with."

"And then what? Are you willing to spend the rest of your life in jail for shooting a judge?"

"Not if I kill myself too."

Chapter 2

"Hold on, you don't want to do that. Think about the families involved. Jyema, think about your husband. How do you think he'll feel if you kill yourself here tonight over my wife? Why don't you put the gun down and we can say that it went off accidentally?" Thomas suggests, walking slowly towards her.

"Just shut up and give me a minute to think," she screams.

I can see Thomas moving towards the door. Jyema is starting to panic more.

"What is there to think about? You made a mistake. Put the damn gun down so I can get to my party."

"It's always about your petty ass. You're still worried about this damn party instead of me. Why couldn't I be what you needed?" she says, starting to cry.

"Are you seriously crying? I don't believe this shit. You got the nerve to stalk me for months and then hold me hostage with a gun and now you're crying?"

"Cam, please just talk to me."

"Talk to you now? You should have asked to talk months ago."

"I did try to talk to you. You kept blowing me off."

"I was busy. You were never my girlfriend, Jyema. What part of that don't you understand? Nothing about the relationship we had should have ended us up here."

"You don't get it, do you?"

"What don't I get?"

Just then Thomas opens the door and the police come swarming in.

"Drop the gun and get down on the ground! Now!"

Thomas and I are pushed out of the room as they scream for Jyema to drop the gun again. We hear one shot and then nothing.

========

"Camille, Camille, what's going on?" I hear my dad saying as he strides towards me.

"Dad, there was a woman in my room when came in to get my earrings."

"What? Who is she? Is it someone you know?"

"Yes, but tonight she was acting really crazy and she had a gun."

"A gun? Did anybody get hurt?"

"I don't know. We heard a shot after the police got us out of there but they won't tell us anything."

Just then the paramedics go past us at the same time security officers come up to me.

"Ma'am, my name is Officer James Moore, head of security. Can you tell me what happened here tonight?"

"Officer Moore, can this wait? There is a very important event going on downstairs in my daughter's honor that she needs to get to. Memphis Police Director Armstrong is downstairs and if I need to call him to handle this, I will."

"No Daddy, please don't call in any favors. Let them do their work. Officer Moore, I've been seeing that young lady but I recently broke it off with her, and tonight she was in my room when I came in."

"Are you pressing charges?"

"Hell yes, she is," Thomas interjects.

"I don't know yet. Can I decide after the party?"

"That will be fine."

"Can you tell me if the young lady is going to be all right?" my dad asks.

"Yes, she'll be fine. She was hit in the leg, only a flesh wound. She will be taken to Medical One and then taken downtown for questioning. Here's my card. Please call me to finish up the report on this as you'll need to go downtown to complete the paperwork if you decide on filing any proper charges."

"Thank you." I turn back to Thomas and my dad. "Can we go now?"

"I cannot believe you are considering not pressing charges," Thomas states angrily.

"I'm thinking about the whole picture, Thomas. The media will have a field day with this."

"I am inclined to agree with Camille on this, son," Dad says. "But let's talk about this after the party."

We make it downstairs to media everywhere. Some were already here for the party and then they got word that shots were fired. The good thing is that my name has not been leaked yet as being involved. Thank God Thomas didn't put the hotel room in our real names.

We get off the elevator and run right into my mother and reporters! They are yelling, trying to get my attention. I put a smile on my face and wave.

"Mrs. Shannon, can we get a picture?"

"Mrs. Shannon, did you hear about shots being fired?"

"How does it feel to be judge?"

"Were you involved in the shooting?"

"Do you have any comments?"

"Camille, boys, where have you all been? Thank God it's an open bar and the live band is good," cries my mom.

"You wouldn't believe me if I told you," I reply.

"Well, smile because there are cameras everywhere. Somebody said something about shots being fired on one of the floors. Did y'all hear anything about that?"

"Kind of. We'll talk about it later," I tell her.

"Camille Holden Shannon!" she utters through clenched teeth, the entire time smiling.

"Not now, Mother!"

Chapter 3

Party Speech

"I cannot believe I am standing here in front of you all as Judge Camille Shannon. Don't get me wrong, I knew it would one day come, but I just didn't think it would be this soon. I must first thank God, He is so amazing. In spite of me and my flaws, He still finds me worthy enough to bless. This past year has been a challenge yet I've made it through.

"I've got to thank my family because without them, I wouldn't be half as strong as I appear to be. Whew, I'm going to try to get through this without crying. To my amazing husband Thomas, even though we go through our struggles because we aren't perfect, you still support me. Thank you for being who I need. My children, Courtney and TJ, thank you for being my strength to go on when I feel like giving up. My parents, Sylvia and Sylvester, you two are the best parents any girl could ask for. You showed me what I could be, how to get there, and even when I make a mistake your love never fails me.

"To my girls Shelby, Ray, Kerri, Chloe and Lyn who isn't here; mere words cannot justify the love I have for you all. You have been the sisters I never had. You pick me up, you push me and you love me despite my shortcomings. You love me through.

"To my Aunt Sara, thank you for being the best auntie ever even though Mom swears all of my bad habits come from you. To my cousin Reese, I do love you and I am so glad you are here.

"To Mr. Thompson, you took me under your wing some ten plus years ago and you've treated me like a daughter. You've nurtured me, taught me and been there for me when I needed a boss and even a father figure. I cannot thank you enough for believing in me. To Judge Alton, thank you for being a great mentor and friend. To my wonderful staff at the law firm, my assistant Stephanie who pushes me beyond my give-up point, and to all my family and friends whom I cannot mention individually, please know that I love you and I thank you for sharing this journey with me.

"This is only the beginning of my destiny. Please continue to pray for me. Now, let's party!"

Chapter 4

As soon as I come down from the stage, I am quickly whisked off to have my photo taken and shake hands. I see my dad talking to Director Armstrong and shake my head. I asked him not to pull any favors.

"There she is, the woman of the hour!" Ray says.

"Oh my God, I am so happy to see you girls!" I say, running to their arms.

"You knew we wouldn't have missed this. And you look gorgeous."

"Thank you."

"What's up? Why are you looking like something is wrong? What happened? Is Lyn here?" Shelby asks.

"No, it's not that. Well, I don't think Lyn is here, but no, it's not her."

"Then what or who has you looking like your cat was killed?" Chloe asks.

"Jyema."

"Jyema?" they all say in unison.

"Shhh…." I say, looking around. "Can y'all get any louder?"

"Please don't tell me you and her are still messing around," Shelby groans. "Cam, I told you to leave that girl alone."

"I know, but it was only once or twice."

"And what happened?"

"She showed up here tonight, um, with a gun," I say, barely managing to get the last part out.

"With a what? Oh, hell no!" Ray screams. "Damn Cam, what are you doing to these chicks?"

I slap her on the arm.

"I didn't do anything to that crazy winch. She's been calling and texting me but I had no idea she was wacko."

"Maybe you need to stop licking them in all the right places," she laughs.

I reach to hit her again and she moves.

"This is not funny," Kerri says. "Was she the reason this place was swarming with police?"

"Yes."

Shelby rolls her eyes. "Dammit Cam. What in the hell am I supposed to tell her husband, my brother-in-law?"

"Look Shelby, I didn't know she would turn out to be a gun-wielding manic. I'm sorry. I should have listened but can you save the 'I told you so' until another day?"

"We won't start at this very moment but we will talk. You can bet your last dollar on that," she responds.

"Hey ladies," Paul says, walking up.

"Paul, I'm glad you came."

"I told you I would be here. Congratulations, you look good as always."

"Thank you. Have you heard from Lyn?"

"Lyn?" Shelby cuts in. "Is she okay?"

"Your guess is as good as mine."

"What do you mean? Aren't you both living in the same house?" Chloe asks.

"She hasn't been home in days. I've been trying to find her and have her committed on a seventy-two-hour hold for observation because something is definitely up with her but I don't know what it is," Paul replies, sighing heavily.

"Damn, I didn't know things were that bad," Kerri adds.

"None of us did."

"Sorry to interrupt but Camille, I need you for pictures," Mom says.

"Sure thing. Paul, don't leave before I get a picture with you."

After another thirty minutes of smiling, hugging and listening to not-so-funny courtroom jokes, I whisper to my mom that I need a quick break. My nerves are on level ten and I need a moment to get myself together.

Walking down the hallway, I am looking down and messing with my dress when someone snatches my arm.

"What the fuck!" I scream.

"Shh!"

"Shh hell! What the f— Charles!"

"I didn't mean to scare you. I saw you walking and you weren't paying attention so I thought I would get you to myself for a minute."

"You scared the shit out of me."

"I'm sorry. You looked like you were in need of this," he says kissing me.

"Hmm," I say, wrapping my hands around his neck.

After a minute of tasting each other's tongues, I push him away. "Okay, okay, stop!"

"I'm just trying to help you," he smiles.

"No, you're not. You are trying to get a quickie."

"Well, since you bought it up…"

"Whatever! Move, I am not about to struggle with this dress."

He takes my hand and rubs it on his growing penis. "You sure?"

"Yes, I don't even know where we are. Somebody can come in and catch us and that's the last thing I need."

"Don't worry, I made sure it's secluded."

"Of course you did. You must have been sure you were getting some?"

"The Bible does say 'ask and you shall receive'."

"Did you really just quote the Bible while you are trying to get inside my panties?"

"Does it help with my case?"

"No."

"Then why are you unbuckling my pants?"

"Because there's no need in letting this go to waste." I slide my dress up enough to squat in front of him. I take all of him into my mouth and then let him slide all the way out, taking time to suck the head extra hard. He grabs the back of my head and I stop and look up at him.

"Don't mess up my hair."

He laughs. Removing him from my mouth, I lick him from the head to the base, taking a moment to suck him in the place that sends shocks through his body. I begin to suck him fast and hard using my hand to help get him there.

"Uh," he moans before grabbing the back of my head again and releasing into my mouth.

I swallow and suck him a few more times before getting up.

"Damn girl!" he says, stepping back. "I've missed you."

"I'm sure you have but I've got to go, sir."

I fix my dress and wipe my mouth before slowly opening the door to make sure no one is in the hallway. I finally find the bathroom, rinse my mouth out and wash my face before returning to the party. That little fix with Charles was exactly what I needed to calm my nerves.

"Hey, where have you been?" Shelby asks as soon as I walk back in.

"I went to the restroom. I needed a minute to myself. Now I need some lip gloss because I can't find my mom with my purse."

"You went to the restroom? By yourself?"

"Yes, mother. I've been doing that for a few years now," I laugh.

"Yea, I don't believe that for a second. Anyway, is this thing with Jyema bad?"

"It can potentially be very bad. She had a gun, Shelby, and she fired a shot at Thomas. I don't think I'm going to press charges but I don't know how this is going to end."

"Man, this is screwed up. I don't know what I'm going to tell Brock."

"Why would you need to tell him anything? This doesn't have shit to do with you."

"I know but—"

"But nothing. Let his wife deal with him. Now, where are the other girls? I want to get pictures before Ray sweats her hair out on the dance floor."

After taking pictures with the girls, mingling with the other guests who are still hanging around and holding so many more boring conversations, I'm ready to go up to my room. I didn't get the chance to talk to Paul again but I'll be sure to call him.

"Hey, are we about done?" I ask Mom when I finally catch her.

"Yes, just about everyone is gone now. All that's left now are a few family members. If you want to go on to your room, you can. I can finish up here."

"You sure?"

"Yes, go ahead. I will see you back at the house tomorrow."

"Okay. And Mom, thank you for a wonderful party."

"You're welcome darling. Sleep well."

Chapter 5

Thomas decided to change our rooms and I'm glad he did. Of course, as soon as we walk in, he is ready to talk.

"Can we please do this in the morning, Thomas?"

"Before or after we go to the police station?" he asks sarcastically.

"Whichever you prefer."

"Dammit Camille, do you care about anyone else other than yourself?"

"Are we back on this again?" I ask, slamming my purse down.

"Yes, we are back on this because, once again, we are put in a difficult position that affects our lives because of you. I told you that you needed to take this stalking thing serious and you never did. I told you to get your life together yet you still take this shit as a joke. Now look at this mess!"

"I didn't tell that crazy motherfucker to get caught up in her feelings, come here with a gun and do all that! Don't blame me for what someone else does."

Slamming a glass down, he raises his voice. "We are in another fucked-up situation because of you. Do you ever take responsibility for what you do?"

"Yes, all the time."

"So, this was not your fault?"

"My only fault was getting involved with her."

"And that's all you got out of this entire mess? You don't take blame for me or you almost being killed or, hell, even for your career as a judge being ruined before it begins?"

"How can I take blame for someone else's actions, Thomas? I didn't make Jyema do this?"

"Man, you are something else." He shakes his head. "Am I not enough for you?"

"Sometimes."

"Wow."

"Are you seriously shocked by my answer?"

"Yes, I am. Shouldn't I be? I am your husband and I should be all you need. Wouldn't you be surprised if I said you weren't enough for me?"

"Yes, because I give you everything you need and could possibly want, yet look at how that turned out."

"What do you mean?"

"You still turned to Chelle."

"Yea, you give me everything I need and want sexually but I turned to Chelle because she was giving me everything else."

"Oh really?"

Just then there's a knock at the door and Thomas goes to answer it while I go into the bathroom. I leave the door cracked open to listen to the conversation

"Good evening, Mr. Shannon. I'm sorry to bother you but is your wife available?"

"What is this about?"

"Sir, this is Detective Craig Harris with the Memphis Police Department and we are here due to the incident earlier tonight. May we come in?"

"Sure, but I thought we were handling this in the morning."

"Yes sir, but your father-in-law, Mr. Holden—"

"Say no more," Thomas sighs. "My wife will be right out."

"While we wait for your wife, can we ask you a few questions?" Detective Harris inquires.

"Go ahead."

"Do you know the assailant, Jyema James?"

"Yes. Well, she is the sister-in-law of one of our friends. I don't know a lot about her but she seemed cool."

"What is the relationship between her and your wife?"

"You will have to ask my wife."

"Ask me what?" I demand, as I come out.

Chapter 6

"Good evening Mrs. Shannon, we are here in regards to the incident earlier."

"Detective Harris, how are you?" I ask when I finally look up from tying my robe.

"Mrs. Shannon, I'm good. Congratulations on your recent appointment. I'm pleased the last issue we dealt with didn't affect it."

"You two know each other?" Thomas asks, looking salty.

"Yeah. Now, what can I do for you, gentlemen?"

"We wanted to ask a few questions about Jyema James."

"I thought we were going to handle this in the morning." I repeat what Thomas said earlier, even though I know what they're going to say.

"Well, your father asked that this be taken care of quietly so we are trying to get it put to rest before the media gets wind of it."

"I told him to stay out of it," I reply, sighing.

"He's a father who wants to protect his daughter. Now, Mrs. Shannon—"

"Please call me Cam."

"Cam, can you tell me about your relationship with Mrs. James?"

"It was only sex," I answer nonchalantly.

Officer Moore glances at Thomas with a shocked look.

"That was my reaction too," Thomas says with an attitude before walking to the bar.

"Um, okay." Detective Harris clears his throat. "What happened here tonight?"

"I came to the room because I forgot my earrings. Jyema was already waiting in the dark when I walked in. I didn't know who it was at first because I couldn't make out the voice."

"Did you see the gun right away?" Officer Moore asks.

"No, she didn't pull it out until later and, again, it was dark so I didn't know who it was or that she had a gun until she turned the lights on."

"What was she doing the entire time?"

"Talking crazy."

"What was she saying?"

"Things like I made her fall in love with me then I cut her off, blah blah. She wanted me to leave with her."

"Mr. Shannon, how did you end up in the room?"

"After Camille was gone for a while, I came to check on her."

"Yea, Thomas surprised her when he came in so she shot at him."

"Are you going to press charges?"

When I didn't answer right away, Thomas did.

"Hell yes we are. That lady is crazy and she belongs in jail. She doesn't care about anyone else but herself and my wife apparently, so yes, we will be pressing charges."

"Thomas listen, this could be bad for me. If I press charges, it could possibly ruin my career before I've even had a chance to sit on the bench."

"Camille, this lady has been stalking you for months and now you want to let her off Scot free? I think not. Let your publicist handle your career, that's what she gets paid for, but we will be pressing charges."

"Wait, she's been stalking you?" Detective Harris cuts in.

"Yes, for about six months. She was trying to keep me from getting the appointment."

"How did you know it was her?"

"I didn't until tonight."

"Okay. This is what we needed to get the ball rolling," Detective Harris says, standing up to leave. "Look, I don't know what you're going to do but come down to the station tomorrow and we can discuss it some more with the District Attorney."

"What about Jyema? Is she in jail?"

"Yes, she was transferred from Regional One and she's in custody. She won't go before the judge until Monday."

"Thank you Detective Harris and Officer Moore. I really appreciate your help on this."

"No problem. You have my card. Please call me if you think of anything that may be beneficial. I'll see you tomorrow."

"Why do you feel the need to keep secrets?" Thomas asks after walking the officers out.

"Just because I don't tell you everything I do, it doesn't mean I'm keeping secrets only that I am keeping it to myself. Can you honestly say you would have dealt with all of this had I told you?"

"I don't know but you should have given me the chance. I'm only your husband, but I guess I don't matter when it comes to Cam, huh?"

"I'm apologize Thomas, I—"

"You're always apologizing but you're never sorry."

"I... wait, what?"

"You are never sorry about your actions; you simply apologize to pacify the moment."

"I never meant for this to happen but I am not to blame."

"Of course you're not. When will it ever be different with you? Are you sleeping with the detective too?" Thomas surprises me by asking.

"What?"

"You heard me?"

"Hell no."

"Y'all seemed mighty friendly."

"Dude, I am not about to go there with you. He helped me with that bogus-ass charge Chelle or whoever tried to put on me some months back. That's it."

"Yea, whatever. I don't know why I asked. It's not like I can believe a word that comes out of your mouth anyway."

"Believe what you want. I am not about to continue this senseless-ass conversation with you."

"You don't have to." He grabs his keys and storms out.

After he leaves, I take three small bottles of vodka from the mini bar and down them all. I cannot believe this shit. Just when I think things can't get worse, they do! Jyema was the last person I thought would do this. She was the farthest thought from my mind. *Damn!*

Chapter 7

I wake up to the hotel phone ringing.

"Shit!" I say, after hitting my hand on the night stand trying to find it. "Hello? Hello?"

"Cam, this is Carin."

"Carin, what time is it?"

"It's 6:50AM. I apologize for calling so early but the media has gotten hold of the story about the shooting last night. They are saying you were held hostage by a jilted lover."

"Oh my God! How did this happen? I haven't even decided if I am pressing charges yet!"

"I don't know, but someone leaked it. Don't worry, I'm on it. I just wanted you to be aware. I'll be at your room in an hour."

I throw the phone to the end of the bed and that's when I realize Thomas never came back last night.

Fuck!

After lying there for another twenty minutes, I get up and shower as I try to prepare myself for this firestorm. After dressing, I hear a knock on the door.

"Hey Carin, come in."

"Good morning. I apologize for calling so early but we've got to get ahead of this mess. It is already on every news station.

I've even had a call from the governor's office and Mr. Thompson."

"Man! I was hoping I could get this handled without the media getting it. This is so fucked up!"

"You are definitely right about that."

"What is your plan? I'm sure it was Jyema's attorney who leaked this because I would have done the same thing for my client."

"Are you serious?"

"Think about it. What better way to get your client off than to put the spotlight on the judge she's sleeping with."

"Yeah, that makes sense. Now, where is your head in all of this? Are you planning to press charges?"

"Honestly, I don't know. I wish this was a nightmare I could wake up from."

"Well, you can't. This is real. All you have to do is turn on any news station and you'll see. So get out your feelings and put your big girl panties on."

Damn! I clear my throat from the crow I just ate. "Um, I don't think pressing charges, at this point, will be great for my career."

"I agree. I think we can spin it using the stalking as the forefront. We can counter that she's in love with you and has been following you for months, causing all kinds of problems, and when you wouldn't reciprocate her feelings, she acted on it."

"Do you honestly think that will work? All she has to do is open her mouth and run with a story of a bi-sexual judge with a never-ending appetite for sex."

"This is our best and only option right now, plus if Jyema wants to go free, she'll go along with it. Right now, we have a meeting with the District Attorney this morning, let's see what they have."

"Okay."

"What do you think Thomas will say?"

"I don't know and, at this point, I don't care. I just want this over with."

"Let's hope we can get this resolved quickly. Cam, listen: I can't tell you how to live your life but as your publicist it is my job to handle your affairs, no pun intended, but this shit here is crazy. You're just getting started in your career as a judge and, if you want to stay in this career, you need to back away from the bullshit."

"I hear you."

"I know you hear me but are you listening?"

"Yes."

"Good. Are you still in your therapy sessions?"

"Yes, but what does that have to do with anything?"

"If you have to ask that question, it means that you need to stick with it. Let's go."

Damn! This bitch doesn't bite her tongue and I like it!

Ms. Nice Nasty 2   *Lakisha Johnson*

Chapter 8

We make it to the police station and it's a madhouse.

The media is once again camped outside yelling their questions.

"Judge Shannon, were you held hostage by your gay lover?"

"Judge Shannon, any comment?"

"Judge Shannon, what will Governor Haslam think about this?"

"Judge Shannon, are you resigning your seat?"

"Wow, they're relentless," I say to Carin as we walk into the building.

"That's why it's my job to handle them and your job to keep quiet."

"Don't worry. I have no plans on opening my mouth."

"Good. That's what got us here in the first place."

"Judge Shannon, right this way," Detective Harris says meeting us in the lobby. "This is District Attorney Brent Walker."

"We've met," I say, shaking his hand. "It's good to see you again Brent, although I wish it wasn't under these circumstances. This is my publicist, Carin Shields."

"It's good to see you as well and I couldn't agree with you more. Ms. Shields, it's a pleasure to meet you. This way," he says leading us to a conference room.

"Mrs. Shannon, would you like your publicist to wait outside?" Detective Harris inquires.

"No, she can stay."

"Okay. Let's get started," he responds, turning on a recording device. "This is Detective Harris of the Memphis Police Department. It is the thirteenth of June 2015, 9:05AM. Present in the room are Judge Camille Shannon, DA Brent Walker and Carin Shields. Camille, I only bought you in today to discuss the actions of last night at the Hilton Hotel. You are not under arrest so there is no need for me to read you your rights. Do you understand?"

I nod my head. "Why are you recording?"

"In order to make sure we have everything covered. Now, please respond out loud for the recording."

Sighing, I say, "Yes, I understand."

"Very well. Can you tell me about the events of last night?"

"Last night there was a party planned to celebrate my recent assignment to judge. Before the party began, I remembered that I'd forgotten my earrings upstairs in my makeup bag. When I walked into the room, it was dark and there was someone there."

"Did you know who it was?"

"Not at first. I knew it was a woman but she was trying to disguise her voice."

"When did you realize who it was?"

"When I got ready to walk out the room."

"What happened?"

"I was tired of playing whatever game she was playing so I told her if she wasn't going to show herself, I was leaving."

"What happened next?"

"She turned on the light and I saw that it was Jyema and that she was holding a gun."

"How do you know Mrs. Jyema James?"

"We were friends and occasional lovers."

"Has she ever been violent before?"

"No."

"Last night you mentioned she was stalking you."

"Yea, she told me it was her last night."

"Why do you think she would do all this?" DA Walker asks.

"I ended things with her because she was getting too clingy. I guess this pissed her off so she thought if she blackmailed me, I would resume seeing her to keep her from going to the media. I never thought she would go this far. Hell, it was only a sexual relationship as we both have husbands, nothing more. At least, that's what I thought."

"Did you think she would actually hurt you?" he asks.

"No, she only wanted me to leave with her."

"Why did she fire the gun?"

"Because my husband Thomas came in and it startled her."

"Do you think she is a threat? Be honest, Mrs. Shannon. I understand you need to protect your image but if you are afraid of this woman, speak now. Are you pressing charges?"

"Yes, I believe she is a huge threat but you are right, I have to think about my image and my career and pressing charges can ruin both."

"It's your choice," Detective Harris says. "We are not forcing you to do anything against your will."

"I understand but no, I'm not pressing charges but she has to agree to leave me alone and let this story die."

"Are you sure?"

"Yes. It's the right thing to do."

"Since there are no charges being filed, I have no more questions. This will end our questioning of Judge Camille Shannon."

Once he stops the recording, DA Walker says, "Look Camille, I understand you wanting to protect yourself from the media but you also need to be careful of this woman. She has some problems and you need to keep your eyes open. If she was bold enough to show up at your hotel room last night with lots of people around, she is capable of anything. I will see what I can do about adding a condition on charges being dropped but, in the meantime, I suggest getting an order of protection against her for the stalking."

"I will."

"I'm serious. Do it today before you leave. There's an office down the hall that can help with that."

"When will she be released?"

"Right now she's being held on disorderly conduct and possibly the gun, if she doesn't have a license for it. The earliest she can go before a judge is Monday," the DA responds. "Do not contact her and she should not contact you. If she does, let me or Detective Harris know immediately."

"Thank you all so much for taking care of this so soon. I know my father had something to do with it but I really appreciate it."

"No problem. Take care of yourself and give me a call if I can be of any other assistance."

"Thanks again and DA Walker, please tell your wife I said hello. I hate that you all couldn't make the party last night."

"She hated to miss it too but she had another event taking place that she couldn't get out of. I'm sure she'll be giving you a call."

Chapter 9

When Carin and I leave, I stop by to file the paperwork for the order of protection. I ask that a hearing take place as soon as possible to get this over and done with. I need Jyema to stay away from me and I'm happy to see that she could be ordered to stay away from my home, workplace and from coming around me, period. This is exactly what I need.

After about two hours of questioning and filing the protection order, we finally walk out of the police station and right into chaos.

"Now to deal with the media," I remark grimly to Carin.

"You let me deal with that. Do not make a comment," she says, glaring at me.

"Damn, do they ever give up?" I ask Carin.

"No, it's their job but please allow me to handle them," she responds again as we begin walking towards them.

"Judge Shannon, any comment?"

"Judge Shannon, are the stories true about you having a gay lover?"

"Judge Shannon, are you getting a divorce?"

"This is the first and last statement we will make on this outrageous story. Judge Camille Shannon was confronted in her hotel room last night by someone she considered a friend. No, they are not gay lovers and no, she is not getting a divorce. This young lady has been stalking Judge Shannon for the last six months in the hopes of building a relationship, and when that didn't happen, she started to blackmail her into stepping down from her recent assignment, Judge of the Seventh District. When she realized that wasn't working, she became unhappy and the end result was last night. Now, Judge Shannon is not pressing charges, she simply wants the young lady to get some help. She has filed for an order of protection in the hopes it keeps her away from her. In the meantime, this will not stop Judge Shannon from doing the job she has sworn to do. If there are any other questions, please refer them to my office."

"Judge Shannon, just one question."

"How does your family feel?"

"Judge Shannon, where is your husband? Does he support your decision?"

Hell, that's a good question. Where is my husband?

"Thank you Carin," I tell her as we walk to her car. "Do you mind dropping me off at home?"

"Of course not, and no thanks needed, it's my job."

She points me to her car and we get in.

"Are you sure you're all right?"

"Yea, I'm just ready to put all of this behind me and get on with my life, especially with me officially taking the bench in a couple of months. I cannot afford to mess this up."

"I'm glad you said that because I got a call from Mr. Townsend a few days ago. There are two cases from Judge

Sumner's calendar that need to be closed before the summer calendar begins. But with everything go—"

"No, I'll handle them."

"Are you sure? You will have to go over the case files and be prepared to finalize the cases in a few weeks. Can you do that?"

"Yes. I need the distraction."

"This isn't a distraction, it's somebody's life."

"That's not what I meant but I understand what you're saying."

"Ok," she sighs. "I have the case files with me and I'm only giving them to you because I believe you can handle it. However, you need to get your shit together."

"I hear you."

"I hope so. There are a lot of people counting on you, Cam."

"I know." I sit back in the seat as my phone vibrates with a text from my therapist.

I sigh out loud.

"Everything ok?"

"Yes, it's just my therapist wanting me to come in."

"Well, that's not a bad idea. Have you seen her lately?"

"No."

"You need to."

I send her a text back saying I'll call her tomorrow.

Pulling up to my house, I see cars and I sigh very loud again!

"What's wrong now?"

"My mom and these impromptu visits. The last thing I want is visitors."

"Do you want me to take you back to the hotel?"

"No, I'll be fine. Thank you for the ride and for handling this situation."

"No problem. Give me a call in the morning so we can discuss some things before the court date is given for the order of protection. And Cam, I hope you think about what I said earlier. Now is the time for you to get your life on track, and whatever you need to make that happen, let me know so that I can help."

"I will."

"You keep saying that, now put some action with it. I cannot help you win the battle if you aren't fighting for yourself. You have a lot of people in your corner who are willing to go to bat for you but we won't keep putting the fire out if you keep starting it back up."

"I understand, Carin, and this time I mean it."

"Okay."

"Thanks again and tell Mr. Townsend I'll give him a call later."

Grabbing my bag from the back seat, I prepare to walk into the house to a slew of questions.

Chapter 10

Slowly walking in, all I want to do is get in the shower and crawl into bed but I walk into a crazy house.

"Mom, what are you doing?"

"Making lunch."

"I can see that, but why?"

"Because I wanted to. Where is Thomas?"

"I don't know. I haven't seen him since he left the hotel last night."

"Humph."

"What's that for?"

"You haven't seen your husband since last night and that's not a problem to you?"

"Momma, he's grown."

"So are you, little girl, but your actions lately don't show it."

"What does that mean?"

"We will talk later, missy. The girls are in the living room. Your Aunt Sara will be here in a little bit and then we will eat."

"Ugh, I am not up for company right now."

"Well, you don't have a choice."

"Where are Dad and the kids?"

"He took them out for a while so we can talk."

Fuck! I scream to myself on the way to my room. This is the last thing I need or want right now.

An hour after getting home, I finally emerge from my bedroom. Thomas is still not home but Aunt Sara and my cousin Reese are here, along with Shelby, Ray, Chloe and Kerri.

"Well, if it isn't the star of the hour."

"Don't start, Reese."

"I'm just saying."

"And you heard what I said."

"Stop it, you two. Not today," my mom says.

I roll my eyes as I go hug Aunt Sara and the girls. Before we can begin to eat, someone starts beating on the front door and ringing the doorbell.

"Are you expecting anyone else?" I ask Mom while heading to the door.

"No."

When I finally open the door, Brock comes barging in.

"Brock, what can I do for you?" I ask, rolling my eyes.

"Stop with the games, Cam, you know damn well why I'm here. Please tell me this shit isn't true."

"What shit, Brock?"

"Have you and my wife been fucking this entire time and now she's in jail for trying to kill you?"

"Well, I don't think you can necessarily call it fucking, but yes that's true, and technically she shot at Thomas, not me."

"This isn't a joke!" he screams. "My wife is in jail and you think this shit is funny?"

"First, you need to lower your damn voice in my house. Second, I didn't tell your wife to go off the deep end. Third, if I want to laugh at the crazy-ass situation, I can."

"I cannot believe this shit. How long?"

"How long what?"

"How long have you and my wife been bumping pussies?" he asks, getting loud again.

"Brock?" Shelby says, coming into the living room.

"Shelby." He looks surprised when she and some of the crew come filing into the living room. "Did you know this shit was going on? You've been keeping secrets too?"

"Man, stop acting like you and your wife are the victims in this," I say, getting upset. "You knew Jyema and I were messing around because you used to enjoy the benefits of joining us."

"Well, I'll be!" Mom cries. "I'm going to get more wine."

"This shit is better than The Have and Have Nots," Aunt Sara says.

"Wow," Shelby says. "Talk about keeping secrets."

"Now, Mr. Save-a-Hoe, get the hell out my house acting like you're so concerned about your wife. Where were you while she terrorized me these last six months? You ought to be happy I'm not pressing charges on that crazy bitch. So while you are here whining to me, you ought to be finding out if she's getting a bond on the other charges."

"Fuck you, Cam! You know Jyema doesn't belong in jail."

"Oh, that's where we can agree because she needs to be at Lakeside Mental Hospital but that's not in my control. When she fired shots in a public place, she pretty much signed her own arrest warrant."

"Cam, is there anything you can do?" Shelby asks.

"About what? Getting Jyema out? I just said I didn't press charges. Hell, y'all should be grateful for that. They're holding her on disorderly conduct and, if she doesn't have a license to carry, on gun charges."

"You are a piece of work," Brock growls, walking toward me. "Karma's a bitch, Cam."

"I know, we're best friends. Now, show yourself out."

Chapter 11

I return to the kitchen with my Aunt Sara looking at me and smiling.

"What, Auntie?"

"Yo lil freaky ass been sleeping with that girl and her husband?"

"Yea, a few times."

"Damn, I need some of that shit you on," she says, laughing.

"Sara, stop fueling her fire. She is bad enough by herself," Mom says.

"Look, I didn't do anything to Jyema that would have made her do the stuff she did. She knew at the beginning this was just for fun."

"Just like Lyn," Kerri says.

"What is that supposed to mean?" I ask her.

"Nothing."

"No, obviously there is something you want to say, so say it."

"It's just you never mean for anything to happen, yet trouble always ends up finding you when it comes to a relationship with a woman. Why can't you leave this mess alone?"

"Because it's my life and I haven't hurt anybody. I was in a bad place with Lyn; I made that mistake. This time, I am not taking the blame for this shit and if you think I should, you can kiss my ass."

"Baby, calm down. We are here to help you. Regardless of who is to blame, can't you see that people are being hurt?" Mom asks. "It's not about who caused it, but rather what are you going to do to change it?"

"I can only work on me. Whatever Jyema is going through, that's not my fault."

"Is there any part of this that is?" she asks.

"Yea, that I didn't break it off with her sooner."

"What is your husband saying about all this?" Reese asks when she comes back in from the bathroom.

"Ask him," I snap, getting ready to leave the room.

"Camille Holden Shannon, don't you dare turn your back on me."

"Mom, I'm sorry if you think I should do something else or take the blame for this entire situation. I am already being judged by the media; I don't need it in my own home. You all can show yourself out."

"We are not going anywhere so bring your ass back here," she says, raising her voice. "We are not judging you but we do love you and we wouldn't be true to you if we don't tell you when you're wrong. We don't want to see your career end before it begins."

"Your mom is right," Shelby adds. "We only want the best for you, Cam, and if we consistently sit by and let your life spiral out of control without trying to help you, what kind of friends would we be?"

"My life isn't spiraling out of control."

"Girl, did you not see this foolishness with your picture attached being plastered all over the news today?" my mother demands. "The same picture they used when Governor Haslam put his trust in you to fill this position."

"This wasn't my fault," I say again.

"Dammit, Camille! Open your eyes. You are ruining your life. What happened to you?"

"I was raped!" I screamed. "I was raped and it changed my entire life. Are you all satisfied?"

The room falls quiet as if it has been frozen in time. Finally Aunt Sara speaks.

"Why didn't you tell us?" she asks, coming over to me.

"No, don't do that. I don't need pity," I cry, pushing her hands away.

"I am not pitying you baby, this is called love," she tells me, wrapping her arms around me.

I cry.

"Stop!" I scream, pushing her away again. "Get out and leave me alone! I am sick of everybody trying to tell me how I should be acting, what I should be saying, what I should be doing. I'm sick of it. Just get out, please!"

"Then do something about it." Shelby walks over and grabs my hands. "Stop fighting us, we aren't your enemies. We are here for you."

I collapse to the floor sobbing as they all gather around me and Shelby begins to pray.

"Father, God in Heaven, I come petitioning your throne right now for my friend, my sister; Camille. God, I come on her behalf asking you to heal the brokenness that is consuming her. Let her release the pain from her past and mend her heart from the hurt that is causing her to run from the will you've placed over her life. God, forgive her sins now and give her the strength to turn back to you. Oh God, right now we need you to come and see about her because she is trapped by her transgressions yet we know you are able to destroy chains. Do it now, Father. Search her heart and remove anything that's not like you. Search her surroundings and remove anything or anyone who means her ill will. God, cover and protect her. And as her family and friends, give us strength to love her through this trying time. Give us the means to pull her out of the pit she's in. Do it for her now, Father, like I know you can. We need you to move like only you can, God. And as we touch and agree at this very moment, I submit this prayer as if it is already done. Amen."

Chapter 12

Shelby pulls me up from the floor and everyone engulfs me in a bear hug.

"We love you Camille and we don't want to see you in the mess you're in. There's still time to fix it," my mom says, wiping my tears. "But you've got to want help."

"I know but—"

"There is no 'but', baby. You've got to get your life together because right now it's in chaos and your children and your husband deserve better."

"My children aren't affected by this."

"How in the hell can you say that when every news station is running this story every hour. You need to get your head out the clouds. You aren't the only one this affects, boo," Kerri says.

"What are you afraid of?" Mom asks. "Why didn't you tell us about you being raped?"

"I'm not afraid of anything. And there was nothing you all could do. It happened when I was in law school. I am dealing with it now and I'll fix this mess, but for the time being can we please drop this?"

"Yes, please!" Reese exclaims. "Now that we've had this prayer meeting slash intervention, can we eat?" she asks.

"Reese." Aunt Sara shakes her head.

"What? I'm hungry. And Cam knows that in spite of our rocky relationship I love her and would never want anything bad to happen to her."

"I didn't know that," I say wiping my face.

"Well, I've said it so you know. Now, can we puh-lease eat?"

"Dang girl, if I didn't know any better I'd swear you were pregnant," Mom says to Reese. "You've been in the bathroom fifty times and eating up everything in sight."

When she doesn't respond, I turn to look at her. It's just like Reese to steal the limelight but, at this point, I'm glad she's changing the subject.

"Yes, okay! Yes, I'm pregnant," Reese yells. "Are y'all happy?"

My mom and Aunt Sara scream.

"It's about time," I say to her and she rolls her eyes.

At least there's some good news from today.

We finally eat and drink, *of course,* until late in the evening. By the time everyone leaves and Dad drops the kids off, I am worn out. My parents never stay with us when they come into town. They say they need their own space *and I couldn't agree more.* I finally finish cleaning the kitchen, double checking the locks and turning out all of the lights when my phone vibrates in my pocket. I don't even bother to look at it because it's probably Thomas whom I haven't seen or heard from since he stormed out of the hotel, and I'm not in the mood to argue.

Finally able to climb into my bed, my phone vibrates again. This time I look at it.

"Yea," I answer.

"Is this Mrs. Camille Shannon?"

"Yes. Who is this?"

"My name is Dr. Talia and I am the attending physician at Medical One Hospital. I'm calling to inform you that your husband has been in an accident."

"Ma'am, I've had a very long two days. Please tell me this is a joke."

"Is your husband Thomas Shannon?"

"Yes."

"I can assure you this is not a joke. Your husband was involved in a serious car accident. We need you to come down to Medical One trauma unit."

"I'm on my way."

I leave the kids asleep and I call my mom and Shelby on the way to the hospital. It feels like I'm driving 100 mph while beating the steering wheel. *This is all my fault.*

"My name is Camille Shannon and I received a phone call that my husband is here," I tell the receptionist when I make it to the hospital.

"His name?"

"Thomas Shannon."

"Camille." I hear a voice I recognize. My parents are here.

"Dad," I cry, running into his arms. "This is my fault."

"Stop that. This is not the time. What are they saying?"

"I'm waiting for them to tell me where he is."

"Mrs. Shannon, your husband is in the trauma bay. Follow the nurse and she will take you."

Chapter 13

We finally make it to his room and my legs buckle when I see him hooked up to the machines.

"Oh my God, Thomas," I say, running to his bedside.

"Mrs. Shannon, my name is Dr. Talia."

"Doctor, is he going to be all right?"

"Your husband was brought in with massive head trauma. We had to perform emergency surgery. We were able to stabilize him by placing a hole in the top of his head to allow more room for the swelling that is happening inside of his brain. There was a small amount of bleeding that we were able to control but the next few days will be crucial to his recovery. Due to that I've placed him into a medically-induced coma."

"Oh God!" I sob, falling back into my dad.

"How long will he be in a coma, Dr. Talia?" Mom asks.

"We're not sure yet. At least until the swelling goes down. We are hopeful that in a few days the swelling will have stopped and we can wean him off the medicine and he wakes up."

"I don't understand. What happened?" I question.

"He was in a motor vehicle accident. The detective handling the case should be in to answer whatever questions he can," the doctor tells us. "Right now, we will monitor him."

"Is there anything else that can be done for my husband, Dr. Talia?"

"At this point, we're doing all we can. It's a waiting game now. I'll be here for a few more hours. If you need me, let me know."

My mom walks over and hugs me. "Camille, I'm going to go out and get the girls. I'll be right back. Your dad is making phone calls in the hall."

Once she is gone, I sit next to his bed.

"Thomas, baby, you've got to pull through this. Please. I'm sorry for everything; just don't leave me like this."

"Camille," Mom says, coming in. "Shelby and Ray are here."

I look up but I cannot say anything.

"We're here for you, boo," Ray says. "What are the doctors saying?"

My mom replies, "She says he has massive head trauma from a car accident. They operated to relieve some of the swelling but the rest is wait and see."

"Car accident?"

"Yes."

"When, where?"

"We don't know," Mom shrugs. "The detective is supposed to be back soon to give us more information."

"Cam, do you need anything?" Shelby asks, kneeling next to me.

"I don't know," I say wiping the tears. "I left the kids asleep at home. Can someone please be there when they wake up?"

"Of course, your dad and I will take care of them. What do you want us to tell them?"

"Just tell them their dad was in an accident but that he's going to be okay. Let them know I'll call when I can."

"Is there anything else you need?"

"Prayers for my husband to pull through, Shelby."

"We can all handle that," Ray promises.

"Thank you all, but there's no need in staying here tonight. The doctor says it'll be a few days before he wakes up. You all go on home and I'll call if there is any change."

"Are you sure? I can stay with you," Ray offers.

"No, but thank you for offering, I'll see you all tomorrow."

After they leave, I slide my chair closer to the bed to be nearer to Thomas. His breathing is labored and I cannot stop my tears.

"Thomas, I don't know if you can hear me but baby, I'm here. You've got to pull through this. The last few months have been hard but we'll be all right. Do you hear me? I know I haven't been the best wife but I will change, if you just come back to me." Wiping away more tears, I continue. "You met me at a time in my life when I was broken, battered and bruised, yet you refused to take no for an answer and you loved me through it. I am going to do the same for you. I wish a million times over I had been honest with you all those years ago about what happened to me in law school and maybe we wouldn't be in this position. If only I had told you about being raped at law school then—"

Ray sniffs. She has tears streaming down her face. "Ray, I thought you were gone," I say getting up from my seat. "How long have you been standing there?"

"For a few minutes. I came back to make sure you didn't need anything," she says, walking towards me. "This isn't your fault, you know that. right?"

"I know but I can't help but feel this way."

"Why didn't you tell any of us you'd been raped?"

"Before today, I'd never told anyone besides my therapist Dr. Scott," I say a little above a whisper. "I was so ashamed."

"Oh boo. You've been holding this all this time?" She opens her arms. "Come here."

"I didn't have a choice."

"There's always a choice. Just know we are here for you now. I'll call you in the morning before I come by to see if you need anything."

"Thanks Ray."

When Ray finally leaves, I sit next to Thomas' bedside, lay my head on his hand and I say a prayer to God for healing and I ask Him for forgiveness of this mess I call my life. *Things have got to get better.*

Chapter 14

"Mrs. Shannon. Mrs. Shannon."

"Hmm?" I grumble when I feel someone nudging me.

"Mrs. Shannon."

"Yes," I answer as I wake up to see Detective Harris with another man.

"I apologize for waking you."

Looking around, I almost forget where I am. I'd been hoping all of this was a horrible nightmare but looking at Thomas lying in the hospital bed, reality sets in.

Sitting up in the chair, straightening my clothes and trying to fix my hair, I say, "Detective Harris, what are you doing here?"

"Is there somewhere we can talk?"

"We can talk here. I don't want to miss the doctor."

"This is Detective Greer and he is assigned to investigate your husband's accident."

"Okay? Why is there a detective assigned? Do you think Jyema had anything to do with his accident?"

"No, we know she didn't have anything to do with it," Detective Greer says.

"Okay," I nod, looking at him. "Then what's going on, Detectives? Was my husband's accident not an actual accident?"

"Yes, it was an accident but—"

"But what?" I ask, getting defensive. "Look Detective, just spit it out. What happened?"

"Do you know a Michelle Craft?"

"Yea, but what does she have to do with this?"

"She was the other person in the car."

"Other person? What do you mean?" I ask, sitting back in the chair and crossing my arms across my chest.

"She was in the truck with your husband," explains Detective Greer.

I laugh, "Really?"

"Yes ma'am."

"So what happened?"

"Apparently, there was a struggle of some sort inside of the truck that caused your husband to lose control. He crossed the median and flipped into an empty field."

"So, you're saying the reason my husband is laid up in ICU in a medically-induced coma is because he and his side chick were fighting inside of his truck?"

"It looks that way," Detective Harris says.

"Wow. So, what were they fighting about? Did Chelle say?"

"No ma'am."

"Figures. That's just like her."

Detective Greer gives Detective Harris a look.

"What aren't you telling me?" I ask.

"Mrs. Shannon, she didn't survive."

"Wait, what?"

"She died at the scene."

I turn to look at him. "What about the baby?"

"What baby?" they both ask.

=========

I'm sitting in a chair next to the window, still trying to wrap my head around the conversation with Detectives Harris and Greer. *Chelle wasn't pregnant.* I cannot believe this.

According to the detectives, there was no evidence of Chelle being pregnant at the scene but the medical examiner would do further testing. This just doesn't make sense when she was supposed to be at least six months pregnant. Now I have more questions than answers and, at this moment, the one person to answer them is Thomas and he's in a coma.

"Hey, are you all right?" Ray asks walking in with a cup of coffee that I desperately need. "I've called your name three times. Has Thomas' condition changed?"

"No," I tell her as I reach for the cup of coffee.

"Then what has you zoned out?"

"The conversation I just had with Detective Harris and Detective Greer."

"What did they say?"

I give her this look because I don't understand the shit to even explain it.

"Cam?"

"Girl," I say laughing, "I know I've fucked up but why is God punishing me?"

"Stop talking crazy, Cam. I don't care if you only go to church three times a year; you know God doesn't work that way."

"It sure feels like it."

"What's going on? What did the detectives say?"

"Um, that Thomas and Chelle were together in his truck when the accident happened."

"Baby momma Chelle?"

"Yes but hold up, there's more. Apparently there was a fight while Thomas was driving that caused him to lose control, cross the median and flip. And get this, she wasn't pregnant."

"Wait a freaking minute. The bitch was lying? Where is she?"

"I'm guessing the morgue."

"The morg—she's dead?"

"Who's dead?" Mom asks walking in.

Chapter 15

"Chelle."

"Chelle? Chelle who?"

"Thomas' baby momma," my dad chimes in. "What happened to her?"

"She was in the truck with him."

My mom stands there with her mouth open.

"And she wasn't pregnant," Ray adds.

"You know, I couldn't make this type of shit up if I was writing a book," I mutter, starting to pace. "Why in the hell were Thomas and Chelle together? This doesn't make sense."

"Calm down." My dad pulls me into his arms.

"Dad, this doesn't make sense!" I sob. "Why were they together? Why were they fighting? Why is this happening? I can't lose him!"

His arms become tighter and he lets me cry. Then he releases me and grabs my face, looking into my eyes.

"Now that you've got that out the way, pull it together. You have to remain strong even at this moment because Thomas will need your strength to make it through. You can't be a hot mess while he is lying here trying to recover. I know you're hurting and you want answers but now is not the time. This is the time for you to put things into perspective and get your life together. God is giving you another opportunity by sparing your husband's life, so don't take it for granted."

"I know but—"

"There are no buts, Camille. Get your shit together." He then kisses me on the forehead, grabs his paper and says, "I have a few phone calls to make and then your mom and I will be back. Call if you need us."

I look at Ray and she shrugs her shoulders.

"You heard the man. Get your shit together."

Just then the doctor walks in.

"Good morning, Mrs. Shannon."

"Dr. Talia, has there been any change?"

"We're going to take him for an MRI to check the swelling and to make sure there isn't any bleeding. It's my hope the swelling has stopped. If it has then we are moving in the right direction."

"What about the medicine you have him on?"

"He's currently on an antibiotic to ensure he doesn't get an infection, a diuretic to reduce the amount of fluid in his body and anti-seizure medicine to make sure his brain doesn't begin to have seizures, which is common within the first week of brain injury."

"Is there anything I can do?"

"Pray. It always helps. The MRI and additional tests will take up to an hour and a half. Go home for a shower and some food. If there's any change, we will call you."

"Thank you, Dr. Talia."

"Come on," Ray says, grabbing my purse, "let's get you home."

"Don't you have to get back to work?"

"Girl, you do know I'm sleeping with the boss, right? Let's go."

We walk out of the hospital room and right into ...

"Lyn? Ray, is that Lyn?"

"I think it is."

"Lyn, wait!" I run up behind her. "Lyn!"

Catching her before she makes it to the elevator, I grab her arm. "Please stop." Trying to catch my breath, I just look at her. "Why are you running from me?"

She doesn't say anything.

"Lyn, answer us. Why are you running? What's going on?" Ray asks.

"I, uh, I heard about Thomas so I wanted to come and check on him, but I didn't want to see any of you."

"Why not? Why are you avoiding us?"

"I have to go."

"No, you're not going anywhere until you answer my question. Why are you avoiding us?"

"I'm not," she stutters.

"Stop lying, Lyn. Look at you. It looks like you've lost weight and haven't eaten or showered in days. Where are you staying?"

"I'm fine; I came to check on Thomas. Can I please just go?"

"You're coming home with me to shower and get something to eat."

"No Cam, I can't."

"I am not taking no for an answer."

Chapter 16

Ray drives and we finally make it to my house. Lyn falls asleep in the back seat of the car and I text Paul to let him know she's with us. I don't tell her what I'm doing because I don't need her to freak out and I definitely don't want her to run. I also text Shelby to fill her in on the latest of both Lyn and Thomas and to let her know I'll call the kids as soon as I shower.

Arriving at the house, I wake Lyn up to get her inside.

"You're ok; I was just letting you know we're at my house. Come on inside," I tell her when she looks confused.

"Lyn, are you all right? What's wrong?" Ray asks as we're walking inside.

"Nothing, I shouldn't be here."

"Yes, you should. So stop acting like you don't know us," I tell her. "We are really worried about you. Please just come inside and take a shower while I fix some lunch. You look like you could use some more sleep. Please," I beg her.

Once inside she is holding on to her sweater like she is a stranger to us. It's crazy. She doesn't seem like the same person we've known for almost ten years.

"Come on and I'll get you settled in the guest room."

When I come back out, I find Paul in the kitchen with Ray.

"Camille, thank you for calling me. Is she all right?" he asks looking like he ran all the way here.

Walking over and giving him a hug, I reply, "No Paul, something is definitely wrong but I don't know what it is."

"Man, I knew it," he sighs.

"You knew what?"

"That something is going on with her. The Lyn we all know wouldn't just up and disappear. Something is not right."

"I know. Hopefully she will tell us."

"Cam, why don't you go and take a shower. I've already called and ordered some Chinese."

"Okay, I won't be long. I want to be done before Lyn is."

I quickly run down the hall to our bedroom and find a change of clothes before taking a quick shower. Fixing my hair and makeup, I'm about done when I hear screaming.

"Paul, what are you doing here? I knew I never should have come here!"

"Lyn, calm down. I'm only here because I love you."

"Love can't fix this! Just let me go!"

"What do you mean? Fix what?"

"You're not making sense. Calm down, Lyn. What are you talking about?" Ray asks.

"Just leave me alone! Why don't all of y'all leave me alone?"

"Lyn," I say coming down the hall, "we are here to help you. Tell us what we can do."

"Just leave me alone."

"Besides that," Paul says. "Because we are not doing that. You owe me more than that. I'm your husband. You owe

Kelsey more than that too. You do remember Kelsey, your daughter?"

"Why do you think I left? I don't want to hurt you or her."

"Hurt us how? What do you mean? You aren't making sense."

"I can't be your wife anymore, Paul, so just let me go, please. Just let me go."

"Why?"

"Lyn, what the fuck is going on? Stop with all the games. Just tell us please," I insist.

"I'm dying!" she yells.

"You're… what?" Paul stammers taking his hands off of her.

"I'm dying," Lyn answers between sobs.

"Dying? Do you have cancer? Do you need a new heart or a liver or something?" Ray questions.

She doesn't respond.

"Answer us, Lyn!" I scream.

"I have HIV."

I fall back into the bar stool as Paul stands there in shock.

The doorbell rings but nobody moves. After a minute or three, it rings again.

Ray finally goes to answer it. She comes back with the food but no one has an appetite now.

"You have… what?" Paul finally asks.

"I'm HIV positive."

"How?" I ask, barely above a whisper.

"From Xavier."

"Who?" Paul demands to know.

"He was a delivery driver at the store."

"Oh my God! How long have you known?" I ask her.

"I found out when I went for my yearly checkup six months ago."

"But why couldn't you tell us instead of running off?" I demand.

"I didn't know how to face you all, especially Paul."

"Oh, now you're worried about me? Were you concerned about me when you were getting HIV and possibly infecting me with it?"

"Infecting you with it?" she says angrily. "We haven't had sex in almost a year, you'll be fine."

"You better hope so," Paul says before storming out.

Chapter 17

"Lyn, have you been to the doctor? Are you taking medicine? What's going on?"

"I don't know," she sobs.

"What do you mean?"

"I haven't been back since I found out?"

"What?" Ray yells. "You're giving yourself a death sentence. This is crazy, Lyn. Just because you've been diagnosed, it doesn't mean you're going to die. There are plenty of people living with this disease."

"But not people like me."

"People like you? People like you? What in the fuck does that mean?" Ray explodes.

"I have a husband and a daughter, a career, friends and everything going for myself. I was not supposed to get HIV. Now look at me. I can't live with this disease. Who would want to be with me?"

"What you become after your diagnosis is your choice. You can still be the same person you've always been. Instead you push away your husband, your daughter, your friends and then you just up and walk away from your business. A business you've wanted all your life. Did you honestly think we would turn our back on you?"

"I don't know what I expected. I just don't think I could live with this."

"Haven't you been living with it the last six months?"

"Yes, but it's not the same. I don't want to be around anyone, I don't want to go anywhere and this is no way to live."

"But you made that choice."

"I know, so please stop yelling at me."

"I apologize for yelling," Ray says, calming down, "but you're being selfish."

"Lyn, we're just upset at how you've handled everything. Your daughter has been worried sick about you. What are you going to do now?" I add.

"I don't know. I need to talk to Kelsey."

"Yes you do, and you need to go back to the doctor and get on a treatment plan. Then you need to pick up the pieces of your life and get back on track. This shit you've been doing, running away, it stops now."

"But—"

"I was told there is no 'but' when it comes to getting your life together. So suck this shit up and deal with it."

"That's right," Ray chimes in. "We are here for you Lyn."

"Thank you."

"There's no need to thank us, we're family. Now, I need to get back to the hospital but can I ask you a question before we go?" I take Lyn's hand.

"Sure."

"Why were you following me?"

"Honestly, I wanted to reach out to you for help but I didn't know how. I was lost after I left the doctor that day."

"But why didn't you come to me?"

"Because I always seem to mess up when it comes to talking to you."

"Last question," I tell her as I pick up my purse. "I thought you were done with Xavier, so how in the hell did you end up back with him?"

"He started delivering to my store again and we picked up right where we left off. Then one day his baby momma shows up and I thought she was coming to show her ass like she used to, and I wish she had. Unfortunately for me, she was coming to share the news that she'd tested positive for HIV. A few days later, I got the call from my doctor to come into the office to discuss the results of the tests from my annual. By the time I left, I was devastated."

"Have you seen him?"

"Oh yea, when I tried to beat his fucking face in."

Riding back to the hospital, Lyn fills us in on the story. She said Xavier showed up to her store to make a delivery, having no clue his baby momma had been there or that Lyn had been to the doctor. By the time the police arrived, she had beaten him unconscious. He refused to file charges but she didn't. Apparently he's known his status for years. *Nasty bastard.*

========

Reaching Thomas' room, I see more nurses and doctors than normal.

"Dr. Talia, what's happening?" I ask nervously.

"Mrs. Shannon, everything is okay. We are just getting him back comfortable in the bed. This is Dr. Rodriguez, the head neurologist on staff, and Dr. Simmons, an internal medicine doctor; they stopped by while making rounds."

"Were there any problems with the MRI?"

"No, there was no bleeding and although there is still some swelling, it's improving. We're going to leave him in the coma a few more days and if there are no significant changes, we will decrease the medicine in order to give him the opportunity to wake up on his own. Once that happens, we can better determine our next course of treatment."

"What are you hoping for after he wakes up?"

"It is our hope there are no residual effects from the brain damage, that he does not begin to have seizures and that the swelling continues to go down. If everything goes to plan, we can then talk about therapy."

"Thank you, Dr. Talia, for all of your help. Is there anything else that can be done?"

"You're welcome, and no, ma'am. All we can do is wait. I will check in on you during my rounds in the morning."

After about an hour, Thomas' room has finally settled down. Mom and Dad stopped by but have now gone. I Facetime with the kids to ensure them that everything is going to be fine.

I curl up in my makeshift sleeping post next to his bed. It's hard to wrap my head around everything that has happened in the last few days. Sitting here watching him sleep while listening to the sounds of the machines, my mind drifts to Lyn and what she is dealing with. I cannot imagine how drastically her life has changed. It makes me realize, even more, that it's time for me to deal with the issues of my past.

I grab his hand. "Thomas baby, I don't know if you can hear this but please come back to me. I know our lives have been chaotic these past months, hell the past year, but it wouldn't be the same without you. You are probably tired of hearing me talk but do you remember when we first met and I kept trying to ignore you and you wouldn't take no for an answer? Remember how persistent you were then? Do you remember how broken I was and you loved me through it? Well, I am right here and I will love you through this. You even loved me enough to make me see that I could love someone else when I didn't think it was possible. There are a lot of things I need to tell you, a lot of things I need to make right with you and I promise you I will; you just have to wake up."

Chapter 18

Two days later – Therapy session

"Camille, it's good to see you today," Dr. Scott says.

"I don't have a lot of time because I've got to get back to the hospital. Can we get on with it?"

"How is your husband?"

"He's stable for now."

"And how have you been since our last session? Did you get a chance to tell your husband about the rape?"

"No, I didn't get the chance before his accident. I did tell my family though."

"How did they react?"

"They were hurt that I hadn't told them before."

"Do you feel better now that you've shared that part of your past with them?"

"Honestly, I haven't had a chance to allow it to sink in. With Thomas' accident and this mess with Jyema, my life is a little more chaotic than normal."

"I heard about the recent event, it was all over the news. Now, Jyema was the woman you were sleeping with, right?"

"Yea."

"Why did she show up that night?"

"Because she's a fucking psychopath."

"It has to be more than that."

"She honestly thought I would leave with her."

"But why would she think that?"

"How in the hell should I know? Didn't I just tell you she's psycho?"

"You've been sleeping with her, right?"

"Yea, what does that have to do with anything?"

"Shouldn't you have known she was psycho?"

"Do you know everything about the people you sleep with? Haven't you heard of wolves in sheep's clothing? Damn, today must be the day for crazy-ass questions. I don't have time for this. I need to get back to the hospital."

"Why do you always run when you are faced with something you don't want to deal with?"

"I'm not running. I'm just tired of these ridiculous questions. Do you honestly think I would have slept with her had I known she was crazy."

"With your 'I am not hurting anyone' mentality, you probably would have."

"What is that supposed to mean?"

"Let's get real, Camille. You only think about yourself during your sex sprees. You don't take into consideration anyone else's feelings because you are like a drug addict looking for your next fix. You will do whatever you have to do to get that high."

"That's your opinion, but I beg to differ because I am not an addict. What I do is nobody's business."

"Tell that to the world who just watched your story on TV."

"I don't know what you want from me. I don't know what you want me to say."

"Say that you need help. Say that you want to be better."

"I've said that," I reply, getting loud.

"Yet you haven't changed and neither have you taken responsibility for your actions."

"What about me needs to be changed, Doc?"

"Your entire life. It's time to grow up and stop being immature."

"So now I'm immature? You just keep the insults coming, don't you?"

"These are not insults, Camille, these are truths. A woman doesn't act like this. You are an addict, and until you recognize and admit it you will continue to spiral. That is, until you hit rock bottom. But you don't have to do that. Help is available."

I laugh.

"What's funny?"

"All of this shit!"

"Why is that?"

"Everybody has an opinion on Cam. Everybody wants to tell me how I should be living and who I should be fucking but it's nobody's business but mine."

"Okay."

"That's all you're going to say?"

"Yes, because you have to get burned before you truly believe the fire is hot. I can tell you over and over again the errors of your ways but unless you see them, all we are doing here is wasting each other's time."

"I couldn't agree more. We *are* wasting each other's time."

"Then you are free to leave, but remember, I'll be here when you come crawling back."

"Yea, don't hold your breath," I snap before walking out of her office.

Chapter 19

Making it back to the hospital, I sit in my usual spot by the window as I watch Thomas sleep, praying today is the day he will be weaned off of the meds and wake up. I can't get the conversation with Dr. Scott out of my head. Maybe I am the reason all this bad shit keeps happening to me, to us. Maybe it's time I stop with all the extracurricular activities. Maybe I—

Someone clearing their throat brings me out of my thoughts.

"So you're the Camille Shannon my sister wanted so badly to be."

"Excuse y—?" I say, turning around to look into the face of a woman who is the spitting image of Chelle, only with shorter hair.

"I look just like her, huh?" she says putting her purse on the table. "I had to come and see for myself this bad motherfucker my sister got herself killed over. I keep trying to picture you in my mind because I can't figure out what you had that would make her want your life so bad."

Composing myself, I start laughing while getting up from my seat. "Baby, I don't know you and I damn sure don't know what possessed you to come here and fuck with me today but I am not in the mood for this shit."

"Let me introduce myself. My name is—"

Blowing because I'm getting agitated, I step a little closer to her. "What part of 'I am not in the mood for this shit' did you not get? I don't care what your name is because you and your sister are the least of my problems right now. The only person I am concerned about is lying right there in that bed. Now, if you will please leave the same way you came in."

I turn to walk back to my chair.

"Wow." She laughs. "You're one cold-hearted bitch. My sister is lying in the morgue and you won't even give me a few minutes of your precious time. She really loved your husband and all she wanted was for him to love her back."

"Oh, is that all?" I ask turning back around. "By faking a pregnancy? Can you see how well that worked out? My husband is lying here in ICU because of your sister and now you want a few minutes of my time? Where were you when she was making our lives a living hell? Why weren't you trying to talk some sense into her then? Maybe your sister wouldn't be in the morgue if you had. Don't blame me for her actions. I didn't fake being pregnant to trap a man, she did."

"She wasn't faking—"

"The detectives beg to differ," I snap, cutting her off.

"She wasn't faking at first. She lost the baby when she was four months pregnant. She fell down the steps in her condo," she replies as tears start to form in her eyes. "Listen, I'm not saying Michelle doesn't have some blame in this but you have some blame in this too, Mrs. Shannon."

"Me?"

"Yes. You were the one that brought my sister into your lives."

"I paid her for a service she provided, it was her job. I can't help what her and my husband did behind my back and I definitely can't help that she fell in love with him. That was her mistake."

"A mistake she paid for with her life."

"Not my fault."

"None of this should have happened."

"I agree with you but this probably could have been avoided had she been honest with Thomas instead of pretending she was still pregnant. I mean, she was constantly popping up at our house and begging him to go the doctor visits with her. What was her endgame?"

"I don't know," she says, raising her voice a little. "I'm sorry but I don't know. I had no idea Michelle was doing all of this. I thought that after her miscarriage she came clean with Thomas. It wasn't until the accident that I found out differently. I went to her house and she had the nursery done and everything. I guess she was too far in by then."

"Well, look where being too far in has gotten us."

"Do you know how the accident happened?" she asks, wiping tears from her face.

"No."

"I talked to Michelle earlier that day and she didn't mention anything about Thomas coming over so I don't know what happened between the time I hung up and the accident."

"Hopefully, he'll wake up soon and tell us."

"Will you please let me know? This has been a nightmare for me and my parents. They are taking her death extremely hard. If it's okay with you, can I leave my card?"

"Sure."

"And again, I'm sorry for coming here. This is something I wouldn't wish on anyone. I will be praying for your husband."

I take her card. "Thank you, and please know your family has my condolences. There was a time I liked Chelle, she was very cool. I hate that things ended the way they did. If there is anything we can do for your family, let me know."

"Thank you," she replies before leaving.

I look at her card. *Nichelle Wilson. Chelle has a twin, DAMN!*

I walk over to his bed and rub on Thomas' hand. "Babe, shit just keeps getting better." I laugh before putting my tablet down to take a walk.

Chapter 20

Coming back down the hall, I see the nurse along with Dr. Talia going into Thomas' room.

"Dr. Talia, is everything ok? What's happening?" I hurry to catch them up.

"Mrs. Shannon, everything is fine. We are lowering the medication that is keeping him in the comatose state. Dr. Rodriguez, the head neurologist, has viewed his latest MRI and test results and feels he can come out of the coma. But please understand, just because there is no bleeding and no more swelling we cannot determine when he will wake up."

Sighing I ask, "I know you have to wait until he wakes up, to know for sure, but do you think there is a chance he'll have brain damage?"

"I cannot say for sure and I don't want to give you any false hope. With any head injury, the effects of the damage differ from person to person. All I can tell you is be patient."

"Thank you, Dr. Talia."

"You're welcome. I'll be back in a few hours to check on him."

I send a text to my parents and the girls to update them on what's going on. I get settled in my chair to go over the case files Carin gave me when Mr. Townsend walks in.

"Mr. Townsend, how are you?" I ask, getting up to give him a hug.

"I am good. How are you faring?"

"As well as can be expected," I reply.

"Come take a walk with me." He reaches out his arm for me to take.

"Is everything all right?"

"Yes, I just want to talk to you to see where your head is. Carin told me she gave you the files for the two cases that need closing out. Are you sure you're up to handling them, because they can be given to another judge?"

"I'm sure. I can actually use the distraction."

"I'm glad to hear it. Another thing I want to discuss is this mess that's been in the news."

"I'm taking care of it."

"I'm sure you are but I am worried about how this could potentially affect your career. Governor Haslam put a lot of confidence in you and the last thing he needs is bad press from someone who was his number one choice."

"I know, Mr. Townsend. You also put your confidence in me and I am so sorry I've let you down."

"You didn't let me down but you are letting yourself down. You know as well as I do the media can't wait to rip apart a successful black woman, especially one who has just been sworn in to take over a position most people wanted Judge Sumner's son to fill. And here you are opening the door and inviting them in to the skeletons in your closet. You may as well have called a press conference."

"It was not my intentions for any of this to happen. I don't want to embarrass myself, your office or Governor Haslam."

"Then you need to decide if this is what you want. I cannot tell you how to handle your personal affairs, but when it begins to affect your career I wouldn't be much of a godfather if I allowed you to crash and burn without giving you some guidance. That's why I hired Carin but there is only so much she can do. You have to help her."

"I understand."

"Do you? This is your career but you have to decide if your personal desires are more important. If they are, you need to step down."

I'm speechless.

"Think about it." He kisses me on the cheek. "I'm going to let you get back to your husband but call me if there is anything you need."

He doesn't even let me respond before he turns to leave.

Walking back down the hall lost in my feelings after that reality check, I see nurses running into Thomas' room.

"Oh my God," I cry out when I hurry in to see him struggling, which means he's waking up.

"Mrs. Shannon, please give us a few minutes to calm him down and for the doctor to check him," a nurse says as she prevents me from getting to his bedside.

My hands are shaking as I pace back and forth. *Please God, let him be okay.*

"Mr. Shannon, calm down," Dr. Talia says. "You're in the hospital. I need you to calm down or I will have to give you something to sedate you. Mr. Shannon, can you hear me? I need you to calm down."

After a few more minutes, she motions for the nurse to give him something through his IV. Once he stops struggling she walks over to me.

"Dr. Talia, what's wrong with him?"

"He has a lot of medicine in his system and he's agitated but I've given him something to calm him down. It's going to make him sleep but I'll be back in a little while to check on him. Why don't you try and rest."

I slowly walk back into the room and Thomas is asleep again.

Just then Ray comes in. "Hey, are you ok?"

"Yea. He woke up but he was too agitated so Dr. Talia gave him something to rest," I tell her, wiping my tears.

"That's good news, right?"

"Yea, but what if he wakes up and he isn't himself? What if he wakes up and can't do anything on his own? Am I selfish for wanting my husband back the way he was?"

"No, that sounds just like you: caring for nobody but your damn self," Jyema remarks, strolling in.

"Bitch, unless you want to be lying in Room 12 down the hall, I suggest you walk your ugly ass right back out of here," Ray declares jumping up.

"Who are you, her next one?" Jyema laughs, looking Ray up and down.

"No, hoe, I'm the only one. Now, get the fuck out!"

Continuing to laugh, she turns and says, "I'll see you again, Cam."

"The nerve of that boot-mouth bitch," Ray fumes, now pacing. "She has the audacity to show up here? I should chase the hoe down and put my foot in her ass. What did you ever see in her anyway?"

"Ray, calm down," I say, standing up to grab her arm. "She is the least of my concerns right now, and I'll let the police handle her. I don't have the time or the patience to deal with her anymore."

"Well, I don't have nothing but time, and if she turns up here again, I'll show her."

Smiling, I say, "Come on, Kung Fu Ray."

"I'm for real, Cam."

"I know you are."

I call Carin to let her know about Jyema's stunt at the hospital and ask her to call Detective Harris. There is an active order of protection and she has violated it. If the police don't deal with it, I know Ray will because she meant every word. I also call Shelby and my parents to let them know about the change in Thomas' condition. I've been trying to prevent the children from seeing him this way but keeping them away now is no longer a choice. Hopefully if he sees them when he wakes up, it'll help.

Chapter 21

The next morning, as I sleep in the bed next to Thomas', I feel something on my hand. I open my eyes to see him looking at me. He's holding my hand.

"Oh my God, Thomas baby. I've never been so happy to see your eyes. Let me get the nurse. Don't worry, I'll be right back."

I run out to the nurses' station and tell them to call Dr. Talia because Thomas is awake. I run back into his room with tears in my eyes.

"The doctor will be here soon. Oh, I am so happy you're here," I say, kissing his forehead.

"Mr. Shannon, I'm glad to see you," Dr. Talia says as she moves to his bedside. "Are you ready to get this tube out?"

He nods.

"As I prepare to remove the tube, I need for you to be very still. It'll only take a few seconds. Do you understand?"

He nods.

"Great. On the count of three, take a deep breath and cough. One, two, three," she says as she removes the tube. "You did great. The nurse is going to give you some water. Sip it very slow because your throat will be sore."

After he takes a few sips, Dr. Talia resumes her check of him.

"Can you cough for me? Good. Take another deep breath. Good. Are you in any pain?"

"A little, my head," he gets out.

"That's to be expected. I'll give you something for the pain. Do you know where you are?"

"Hospital."

"Do you know what year it is?"

"2015."

"And who is the president?"

"Obama."

"Great. We will do another MRI of your head just to make sure everything is okay. If it is, we'll move you to a regular room tomorrow and then rehab in a few days. I'll be back after the test. Don't try to do too much."

"Thank you Dr. Talia. Babe, I am so happy you're awake."

"What happened?"

"You were in an accident."

"When?"

"We can talk about that later, ok? Do you want some more water?"

He shakes his head no.

"Where are the kids?"

"They'll be here in a little while. They cannot wait to see you."

Just then a guy comes in to take him for his MRI.

"It should take about an hour," he says.

"Thanks. I'll be here."

I decide to go over the case files I have in my bag. I only have a few days before I have to preside over them and the last thing I need is to be unprepared.

After about forty-five minutes, I stand to stretch.

"Mrs. Shannon."

"Detective, is everything ok?"

"Yes, I received a call that your husband was awake. I came to see if I can talk to him."

"He'll be back from his MRI soon. Is there an update on the accident?"

"No. I just need to get your husband's statement in order to close the file."

"What about Chelle? Did you verify if she was pregnant or not?"

"No, she wasn't. What gave you the idea that she was?"

"She's been telling us that she is for the last six months."

"What's going on?" Thomas asks as he's wheeled back in.

I wait until he is settled back into his bed.

"Thomas, this is Detective Greer and he is here to get your statement about the accident."

"Okay."

"Mr. Shannon, do you remember anything about the accident?"

"Uh, I remember going to Chelle's house. We were in her living room talking when she started kissing me." He looks over at me.

"Don't stop on my account," I say.

"Things started getting heated. She wasn't paying attention and allowed me to remove her shirt. That's when I saw that she was wearing one of those fake stomachs. I got upset and—"

He stops mid-sentence.

"Mr. Shannon?"

"She was in the truck with me," he finally realizes. "Is she ok?"

Neither of us responds.

"Camille, is she ok?"

"No, she didn't survive the accident."

He lays back on the pillow. "Damn, this shouldn't have happened."

"Mr. Shannon, can you tell me what happened inside the truck?"

"Um, we were arguing about the lie she's been telling the last six months. When I grabbed my phone to call Camille, she flew into a rage. She grabbed the wheel and I don't know what happened after that."

"Thank you Mr. Shannon. That's all I need. I'll leave you alone now to rest but if there is anything that comes up, I'll be in touch"

After the detective leaves, I slide my chair over to him.

"What's wrong?"

"How did I not know she was lying for the last six months? I mean, she was really convincing."

"Well, according to her sister she—"

"Her sister?"

"Oh, Chelle has a twin sister. She stopped by the other day and, according to her, Chelle was pregnant but she lost the baby two months ago but kept up the charade."

"But she had to know I would find out when she didn't have a baby in three months' time."

"Yea, well maybe she thought she could sleep with you and get pregnant again."

"I wouldn't have slept with her."

"You almost did the night of the accident."

"That was because I was mad at you."

"I know, and I am so sorry about all of that. Almost losing you has put a lot of things into perspective."

"I hope so," he says before cringing in pain.

"You ok?"

"My head is killing me all of a sudden."

"Let me call the nurse."

Chapter 22

It's been two weeks since Thomas regained consciousness. He was moved to a rehab and the kids and I have been visiting him every day. I only have a couple days before I report to my new position on the bench and I am glad Thomas is finally getting his strength back. I don't know how I would have been able to do it otherwise.

Walking into the rehab center I run into his new therapist, Dr. Marcus Hilton. I stop to check in with him while sending the kids on to Thomas' room.

"Mrs. Shannon."

"Please call me Camille."

"Camille, how are you today?"

"I'm good Dr. Hilton, how are you?"

"Great. I'm just leaving a session with your husband."

"How is he?"

"Physically he's good, getting stronger by the day. There don't seem to be any effects from the accident that will prevent him getting back to his daily activities in a few weeks. He is still a little weak but using a cane should help with that."

"How can I help him?"

"What you have been doing is great. He really loves you and it shows by his determination to be there on your first day on the bench."

I give him a look.

He chuckles. "It's all he talks about. He is very proud of you."

"And I am proud of him. He has really worked hard these last two weeks."

"That he has and that's why I'm releasing him to go home tomorrow."

"That's the best news I've heard in the last month. Thank you, Dr. Hilton."

"You're welcome. I'll be here tomorrow to release him. How about 10AM?"

"That works great for me."

"See you then."

"Oh, wait." I turn back to the doctor. "Did you already tell Thomas?"

"No, I thought you'd want to deliver the good news."

I walk into the room to see TJ showing Thomas some pictures on his phone. They are laughing and it feels good.

"Hey."

"Mom, look, Dad can walk without his cane."

"Oh really? Dr. Hilton told me you need that cane to walk. Don't hurt yourself trying to be hard."

"Stop being a worry wart, mom," Courtney says.

"Yea Mom," Thomas says mockingly.

"All right, keep it up and you won't be able to come home tomorrow."

"Dad is coming home?" TJ practically shouts.

"Yes."

"'Bout time."

"Courtney!"

"Leave her alone, Camille. She is as tired of this place as I am."

"Can we go to the vending machine?"

"Yes but don't eat too much junk or you won't want a meal when we leave here."

By the time I turn around, Thomas is standing behind me. "Okay, Mr. Macho."

Before I can finish, he pulls me into a kiss.

"Well, ok then," I say, when he finally releases me.

"I'm sorry, I couldn't resist. Your lips look so tempting. How about we fool around in this lit bitty-ass bed."

Without saying anything, I grab and kiss him like it was the last time I would see him.

Stepping back and wiping my mouth, I tell him, "I'll see you in the morning."

"You're really going to leave me like this?"

"Goodnight, Mr. Shannon."

Finally getting home after stopping to eat, I get the kids settled. I pay some bills online and straighten up my home office. *It was a mess.* I head into my bedroom to take a shower.

By the time I am done, I come out to a missed call from Charles.

"Judge Alton, to what do I owe the pleasure?" I ask when he answers my call back.

"Judge Shannon, how are you?"

"I'm great. Where have you been hiding?"

"Just working, trying to clear my calendar before this term ends. I don't usually take cases during the summer months."

"Okay, Mr. Big."

Laughing, he replies, "No, you'll learn soon enough that you have to make time to relax or else the job will consume you. Anyway, I called because I heard you're coming in on Monday to close out Judge Sumner's calendar. Are you ready?"

"As ready as I'll ever be." I laugh. "In all honesty, I need it to clear my head so yes, I am beyond ready."

"That's good. How's your husband?"

"Better, he's coming home tomorrow."

"That's good to hear."

"It is, but I know you didn't call me to talk about my husband."

"Can't an old friend call to check on you?"

"Old friend, huh?"

"Yes."

"Well, thank you for checking on me, old friend. Good night."

"Wait, where are you?"

"I thought so," I say giggling. "Where do I need to be, sir?"

"On your knees with your ass in the air."

"Now you're talking."

"Can you meet me at Residence Inn on Poplar Pike?"

"I can be there in thirty minutes."

"I'll text you the room number."

Chapter 23

Shit, it's been weeks since I've been sexed. Come to think of it, it's been longer than that and after that kiss with Thomas my girl was throbbing for some loving.

Stopping by Courtney's room, I push open her door. "Hey, I have to run out for a little while. I should be back in about an hour. Call me on my cell if you need me."

She nods and replaces her earphones.

========

Pulling up to the room number Charles texted, I reply with a text for him to open the door. I get out the car, almost running, wearing stilettos and a maxi dress with nothing underneath.

He opens the door to let me in and quickly closes it behind me before locking it.

"Hey," I say walking into his arms where our lips lock and my tongue finds his.

"Hmm," he moans when he finally lets go. "You smell so damn good."

"I taste even better," I smile as I walk away from him, pulling my dress over my head.

He laughs. "Only you would come out the house with basically nothing on but heels."

"Putting all that on is wasted time, don't you think?" I ask as I turn my back to him and rub my hand over my butt.

"I'm inclined to agree."

"Have a seat on the side of the bed," I tell him.

He eyes me suspiciously but does what he's told. I pull a chair in front of him and sit, placing my legs on the bed on opposite sides of him. I spread them wide enough to make sure he has a fantastic view of the show.

He moves to touch but I slap his hand. "It's not your turn."

I lick two of my fingers, one at a time, before rubbing them over my shaven candy box.

I smile while watching him squirm. "I enter them into me and begin to pleasure myself."

I use the other hand to spread my lips while I continue to play with my clit.

"Hmmm, she's so wet," I moan to him as he watches me.

"Make that pussy cum," he says, licking his lips.

I spread my legs a little further and begin rubbing harder and faster.

"Mmm, ooo, ooohhhh!!" I scream while the orgasm rocks through me.

He grabs my legs and pulls me from the chair, flipping me on the bed. Working to undo his pants, he quickly steps out of them as he reaches for a condom on the table and covers his rock-hard penis with it.

He pulls me down to the edge of the bed and begins kissing the inside of my thighs. He enters me hard and I feel every inch of him as he slides in and out slowly.

"Faster baby, please," I beg, grabbing his butt.

"You miss this dick?"

"Yes, give it to me."

"How do you want it?"

"Just like that, don't stop."

I spread my legs wider to give him all the access he needs to hit my spot.

"This pussy feels so good."

"Does it?" I moan into his ear. "How good?"

"Damn good," he replies pulling out. "Turn over."

Smiling, I do what I am told and get on all fours.

He spreads my legs and pushes me down. I rub my girl as he works to get me in the position he likes.

He slaps me on my ass as he prepares to enter me. He opens my butt checks and licks my girl before entering her.

"Yes," I moan. "Oh God, yes!"

I grip the bedspread as I begin to give it back to him. He is squeezing my waist and giving me every inch of himself.

"Shit," I scream as another orgasm takes over me.

What is this man doing to me?

I push off of him. "Lie down. Do you have another condom?"

"Yes," he says, breathing hard. "On the table."

"Good."

I pull the condom off and instantly take him into my mouth. Taking all of him in, I come up for air and go right back down, slurping and sucking at the same time.

"Oh," he cries, grabbing the back of my head.

I come up for air again and begin sucking on the head while massaging his balls. I start bobbing faster and harder.

"Shit!" he groans.

I finally release him before getting up to get the other condom. Tearing open the package, I lick him one last time before sliding the condom on.

I straddle him, sliding down onto him. Tightening my muscles, he grabs my hips, which causes me to ride harder. He closes his eyes and starts to pump faster.

I place my hands on his chest as I begin to roll my pelvis in a circular motion.

He finally lets out a moan of some sort and I collapse on his chest.

"Damn girl."

"I guess it's fair to say we've missed each other, huh?" I laugh.

"You're right about that. Do you have to rush home?"

"Not tonight," I tell him.

"Good." He gets up to pull the cover from under me to put over us.

He pulls me into his arms and I don't resist.

Chapter 24

The next morning I walk into Thomas' room to him packing up his bag. "Hey, you ready to go?"

"Yes." He hugs me.

"Hey, you two," Dr. Hilton smiles, walking in. "I have the release papers and the schedule for outpatient therapy."

"Great." I go over to sign.

"Thomas, do you have any questions for me before you leave?"

"No, I think you've covered everything. I'll see you at our next session."

========

"Welcome home," everyone shouts when we walk in.

"Thank you all," Thomas responds. "I am so happy to be surrounded by loving family and friends. I can't wait to take a shower and sleep in my own bed."

"We're just so happy you're home," my mom says giving him a hug.

After about an hour of mingling with the family, everyone goes. I send them home so that Thomas can relax.

The kids are spending the night with Shelby again but I promised her and my mom that I will go to church with them in the morning. Actually, my mom wouldn't take no for an answer. *I can't wait for them to go home!*

I spend a little time cleaning up, making sure the house is locked and the alarm is on. I go into the bedroom and find Thomas pacing.

"Hey, are you ok?"

Without saying anything, he walks over, grabs the back of my head and sticks his tongue in my mouth.

"Hmmm," I say, as I kick off my shoes and start undressing in front of him. I remove my jeans first and then my tank top, leaving only my thong and bra. I take his hand and lead him over to the couch in our room.

I kneel in front of him and start to unbutton his pants.

"Are you sure you're up for this?" I ask as I work to slide them off.

"It's been over a month, what do you think?" he smiles.

"All right, but don't blame me if you end up back in the hospital," I smile, looking up at him while rubbing his penis up and down.

"Oh, I'll definitely go with a smile on my face."

I lick my lips as I suck him into my mouth. I slowly slide him in until I feel him tickling the back of my throat. I slide up and down, fast then slow, slow then fast, allowing my saliva to drip down the sides.

I come up for air and then quickly take him back in before he can even blink.

"Oh shit," he moans, before grabbing my head with both of his hands. "Suck that dick, girl."

I stop and look at him.

"What's wrong?" he asks. "Did I say something wrong?"

I chuckle a little. "No, it's not wrong, but you don't normally talk like this."

"I'm sorry."

"No, I like it." I smile before resuming my position.

I suck him back into my mouth and begin to suck faster and harder.

"Yea, just like that," he says, pushing my head. "Your mouth feels so damn good."

I release him and stand to remove my thong. Stepping out of it, he stands up and kisses me. He moves down to my neck then down to my chest before removing my bra and taking a nipple into his mouth. He moves from one to the other, making my legs weak.

"Hmm," I moan as one of his hands roams down to my candy box. I spread my legs wide enough for him to slide a finger in.

"You're so wet," he whispers in my ear as I gyrate on his hand.

Placing one foot on the ottoman, I give him more access and he instantly inserts another finger into me, causing me to cry out in pleasure.

"I'm cumming, don't stop!" I moan as he covers my mouth with his.

"God!"

He turns me around and I place my hands on the ottoman while he spreads my legs. Rubbing his penis against my opening, he teases me.

"Please!"

"Please what?"

"Stop teasing me."

He enters me hard, pumping faster and faster. I move away from him to slow him down.

"Slow down baby, she's not going anywhere."

He grabs my waist and squeezes while I try to spread my legs a little because it felt like he was touching my chest, plus being with Charles the night before, I'm still sore.

He pushes my legs back together as he continues to pump into me and I can't help but to scream out. The pain along with the orgasmic sensation I feel at that moment sends shivers through me.

"Oh!"

For the first time in forever, I want to hit the damn ottoman and tap out like I was at WWE but I can't. Yes, this shit is feeling good but my insides are sore as crap.

"Ah," he grunts tightening the hold on my waist. "Ah shit!"

He finally releases inside of me before falling back on the couch, pulling me onto him.

"That was amazing," he laughs.

"Care to join me in the shower or are you overly exerted?" I laugh.

"Is that a challenge?"

I smile.

"Game on!" he says chasing me into the bathroom.

Chapter 25

"Last night was amazing," I say to Thomas when I walk into the kitchen where he is already pouring coffee.

"Yes it was." He smiles while setting a cup in front of me.

"What do you have planned for today?"

"Nothing other than lounging around the house. Where are you headed?"

"To church with my parents, Shelby, Derrick and the kids. You want to come?"

"Sure."

"You do?"

"Yea, why do you look surprised?"

"It usually takes a lot more persuasion than that to get you to go."

"Well, last night was enough. Do you have time for me to get dressed?"

"Yea, there's still about forty-five minutes before we need to leave."

We make it to Fellowship Restoration Ministries on time. *For a change.* We meet the family out front and all walk in together. I've been here a lot, and even though they always make you feel welcome, I've never felt comfortable enough to join. I don't know why. Yes, I was raised in church and my parents are avid Baptist worshippers but I haven't had a church to call home since I left for college. I n*ever felt the need to.*

We get to our seats and the praise and worship team opens the service. I can honestly say I don't know the song they are singing because I haven't been listening to anything closely related to gospel lately. Hell, since I'm being truthful, I haven't really been listening to God either. I guess you can say that's why my life is screwed up now.

As they sing, something stirs in my stomach. I can't explain it. No, like I said I am not overly religious, but something about this song is getting to me. I am hanging on to every word they sing because it feels like they are singing directly to me.

I look around and everyone is into the worship service so maybe it's just my crazy ass overreacting. But as they continue to sing, I can't help but listen… intently.

Ok God, what are you trying to tell me?

The song is saying that we belong to God and we should give ourselves to him. I sing along with the congregation. Shelby, who is sitting next to me, grabs my hand.

"You ok?" she asks, leaning over to me.

"Huh?"

"Are you ok?"

"Yea, I'm good."

The service continues and Pastor Ansley gets up to preach. He is preaching on the benefits of waiting.

His scripture comes from Psalm 40:1-3 that says, "I waited patiently for the Lord to help me, and he turned to me and heard my cry. He lifted me out of the pit of despair, out of the mud and the mire. He set my feet on solid ground and steadied me as I walked along. He has given me a new song to sing, a hymn of praise to our God. Many will see what He has done and be amazed. They will put their trust in the Lord. Oh, the joys of those who trust the Lord, who have no confidence in the proud or in those who worship idols."

I look over at Thomas and it looks as though he is on the edge of his seat.

Pastor Ansley continues. "Has anyone here ever cried out to the Lord and it seems like your cries for help fell on deaf ears? Ever felt like you were knocking yet no one answered? Ever felt like you were trapped in a spiritual pit of damnation and the walls were closing in? Ever felt like your feet were trapped, like David says, in mud and mire and every time you try to move it becomes tighter around your ankles? Anyone other than me ever been there?

"Ever paced the floor all night long and still had to work the next day? Have you ever had to figure out how you were going to pay the bill that's due and feed the children too? Anybody? Ever felt like your life is being suffocated by quicksand and the more you move, the harder it becomes to breathe? Had so much hell to show up in your life that it makes you cry out like David, 'Hear my prayer, O LORD! Listen to my cries for help! Don't ignore my tears. For I am your guest — a traveler passing through, as my ancestors were before me!'

"Well, I stopped by this morning to tell you God has heard your cry, my sister. He's heard your cry, my brother, and He's coming but you have to wait. Yea, I know you may be tired of waiting, tired of folk telling you to pray about it, tired of hearing that it'll be all right in the morning yet every time morning comes you're still catching hell, but wait. Yes, I get it; you're tired of being without, tired of making that smile appear genuine, tired of taking aspirin because you can't afford your real pain pills, tired of eating ground beef when you want a steak, tired of asking folk for rides when you want your own stuff, tired of walking in darkness but, baby, wait… For Psalm 27:14 says, 'Wait patiently for the LORD. Be brave and courageous. Yes, wait patiently for the LORD.'"

The church is on fire. The more Pastor Ansley preaches the more Thomas becomes engrossed and, out of nowhere, he is on his feet in the midst of the praise. *Lord, who is this man?*

Pastor Ansley says, "The doors of the church are open. You may come by letter, Christian experience or candidate for baptism. However you choose to come, just know the doors of the church are open for you. Don't wait until it's too late.

It's better to have God and not need Him than to need Him and not have Him. Is there one today?"

Before Pastor can say anything else, Thomas moves from his seat and begins walking down to the front of the church. *What the—!*

"Oh my God, Cam," Shelby gasps, about to shake my arm off. "Is Thomas really joining church?"

"I guess so," I answer through my shock.

"Do you want to go up there?"

"No! I am good right here."

Chapter 26

After Thomas is given the right hand of fellowship, he goes with the church clerk. I am still in disbelief that this has even happened.

Once service is dismissed, I head to the back of the church to wait for him when I run right into Pastor Ansley.

"Sis. Shannon, it's good to see you again. We are so happy that Thomas has finally decided to join us. Now, we are just waiting on you."

"It's good to see you again, Pastor. Service was amazing today," I say, dodging his last sentence.

"Congratulations on your recent appointment to judge. I pray everything will work out for you and your family. Shelby told us about Thomas' accident, and thank God for his healing."

"Thank you Pastor, it has been one he— I mean, it's been a rough year."

He chuckles. "I completely understand. Please let me know if there is anything we can do."

"I definitely will," I reply as he walks off.

"Hey," Thomas says.

"Hey yourself."

"What's that look for?"

"What look?"

"The one you have on your face."

"I'm just surprised at you joining church."

"I was surprised at myself but it was like I couldn't stop once I started walking. It felt good," he says with the biggest smile on his face.

"I am proud of you," I reply giving him a hug.

"Thank you. Where's everybody else?"

"They're meeting us for lunch at Shelby and Derrick's house."

========

After dinner at Shelby's, we finally make it home. I have some preparing to do for my first day as Judge Camille Shannon tomorrow and I'd be lying if I said I wasn't nervous.

The kids are preparing for their week and Thomas is in the den watching TV.

I make it to my office to check my email when my phone rings with a call from Carin.

"Hey Carin, is everything all right?"

"Cam, how are you? Are you ready for tomorrow?"

"Yes, I am but I know that isn't the reason for your call."

"Actually no. I've been talking with the DA about Jyema's case."

"Ookay… Is he going to do anything about her violating the protection order?"

"No."

"No? Why not?"

"That's the thing: I don't know. He is being evasive, which leads me to believe there is something else going on but I don't want you to worry about that. I'll handle it."

"If you say so."

"I'm serious, Cam. Let me handle it. All I need you to do is focus on your first day on the bench tomorrow."

"I hear you, Carin. I'll talk to you later."

"Carin, your publicist?" Thomas asks walking into the office.

"Yea, she's still handling the mess with Jyema. I didn't tell you but she showed up at the hospital when you were there but the DA won't file charges on her violating the protection order."

"That's crazy. According to the law, she should be charged with criminal contempt of court. Have you spoken to the DA?"

"No, I'm trying to let Carin handle it."

"Well, don't wait too long. That Jyema bitch is crazy and she needs to be in jail."

"I won't. If Carin can't get anywhere, I'll go over the DA's head."

"Speaking of head," he says, smiling.

"Stop! I don't have time to fool with you. I have to go over my cases for court tomorrow."

"Come on, you can give me a quickie."

"Man, if you don't move," I say, pushing him off. "Give me an hour and then I'll let you play in candy land."

"Well, hurry up because I have a yearning for something sweet." He licks his lips.

"An hour won't kill you."

"Whatever, party pooper!" he smiles, kissing me on the forehead. "I'll be in the den if you need me."

I like the new Thomas. God, can he please stay? I silently pray.

Chapter 27

First Day on the Bench

I'm excited to be walking into the courthouse today. Even though there are only two cases to close, I am looking forward to it.

"Judge Shannon, it is so nice to finally meet you. I'm Judy, your secretary. Follow me and I will show you to your office. Your robe is already hanging up inside. If you let me know how you want your office decorated, I can take care of it for you but you should find everything you need."

"Whoa Judy, do you ever take a breath?" I ask, stopping her en route.

"Oh yes ma'am, occasionally." She giggles. "Right this way."

She opens the door to my office. *My office.* "Would you like some coffee or some tea? As soon as Rueben gets here, I'll bring him in to meet you. Gina is here somewhere, she'll be in too. Is there anything else you need?"

"Listen baby, you need to give me a minute to answer you. You are asking fifty questions within the same sentence. Now, yes I would love some coffee. No, there isn't anything else I need. And who in the hell are Gina and Rueben?"

Laughing she waves her hand. "My apologies, suga. Gina is a judicial assistant and Rueben is one of the bailiffs. I'll be right back with your coffee."

"Damn," I say to her back as she hurries out the door.

"I see you've met Judy."

I look up to see this nice looking man standing in my doorway.

"Yes, is she always this way?"

"No, she can be worse. Hi, I'm Rueben." He comes over to extend his hand. "I'll be your bailiff."

"Rueben, it is very nice to meet you."

"Likewise. I'm not going to take up anymore of your time. I will let you get settled before court starts. I'll be back about twenty minutes before court begins to grab your things and to walk you out. Is there anything I can do for you in the meantime?"

"Nothing I can think of at the moment. Thank you, though."

I finally sit down at my desk.

"My desk!" I mumble to myself as I rub my hand over it, my computer, the chair and everything else. I guess touching it makes it seem more real.

Blowing out a breath, I pull out the case files and turn on my computer. *Let the fun begin.*

"Here's your coffee," Judy says barging in. "I brought you some cream and sugar. I would normally have it fixed for you but I don't know how you like it yet, but I'll get it down soon enough. Anyway, do you want anything to eat? There's some muffins and fruit. I—"

"Judy!" I scream, realizing I probably said her name a little louder than I expected when she gives me this startled look. "I apologize. I didn't mean to yell but you're talking a mile a minute. Please calm down."

"I'm sorry, suga, I've had two doughnuts and some coffee this morning while I waited for you to come in and it has me a little hyper."

"A little?"

She laughs.

"Please don't do that again and please, please stop calling me ma'am and suga: call me Cam."

"Yes ma'am."

I roll my eyes. She talks so damn fast, I don't think she realized she called me ma'am again.

"Judge Shannon," she continues, "you have one case today which is a divorce case. I'm sure you're up to date with the case file but it's at 10AM. Do you need anything from Gina to assist you before it begins?"

"No, I think I am ok for now but thank you, Judy."

"No problem. Buzz me if you need me."

When she finally leaves, I let out a sigh. She's going to take some getting used to. *For sure!*

=====

"Judge Shannon, are you ready?" Rueben asks as he enters my office.

"Yea, give me one minute," I yell from the bathroom.

Coming out smoothing the wrinkles in the dress, I run right into him.

"I am so sorry, Judge Shannon," he says grabbing my arm.

"No, I apologize. I hadn't even looked up. I was fooling around with this dress. Does it look ok?"

"Yes. It looks great, especially with those shoes."

I give him a look.

"Yes, I know, fashion. Not all men are oblivious to it. My husband and I are huge lovers of fashion."

"Your husband?"

He clears his throat. "Oh, you didn't know? Is that going to be a problem?"

"Does it affect your job?"

"No, of course not."

"Then no, I don't have a problem."

"Are these the files you're taking with you?" he asks.

"Yes, the ones stacked right there on the edge."

"Okay. Then let me explain how it will go. When we go out, I'll call court to order and then it will be in your hands. I will swear in all witnesses as well as handle any additional things you need while court is in session. If there is anyone you feel needs to be removed, let me know and I will take care of it. I am here to ensure your safety and to help anyway I can. Do you have any additional questions?"

"No, I think you've covered everything."

"Please don't hesitate to ask. I'll be outside when you're ready."

"Thanks, I'll be right out."

Chapter 28

I go over to where my robe is hanging and it is finally sinking in. Today, it gets real. I slip the robe on my arms and zip it up. *Game time, Camille.*

"All rise, this court is now in session; the honorable Judge Camille Shannon presiding."

"You may be seated. The court is now in session," I say as I bang my gavel for the first time. *I want to smile so badly but I have to contain myself.*

"Judge, this is case 1785427 of Kandice Tutwiler versus Larry Tutwiler."

"Thank you Rueben. Ms. Kandice Tutwiler, you are seeking to dissolve your marriage on the grounds of infidelity, is that correct?"

"Yes, your honor."

"And it is my understanding no resolution could be reached before trial, is that correct?"

"That is correct, Judge."

"Even with the weeks that you've had in the absence of Judge Sumner, nothing could be resolved through mediation?"

"Unfortunately no, Judge," says Attorney Whitlock, who is representing the plaintiff, Kandice. "We've tried to handle this through mediation but no agreement could be reached."

"Fine, are you ready to present your opening statements?"

"Yes ma'am."

"Then let's begin."

Mr. Whitlock stands up from his chair and begins to speak as he adjusts his suit jacket. "Judge, my client is seeking a divorce from her husband of seven years due to infidelity. She is seeking alimony, full custody of their two daughters, along with child support. We will show proof of the defendant's extra marital affairs as well as the child he produced outside of their marriage. There is also proof of a home and car he has purchased for one of his mistresses. The defendant doesn't deny the affairs but wants the court to believe it is because his wife doesn't fulfill his sexual desires."

I move on to the attorney for the defendant. "Ms. Abernathy, are you ready with your opening statement?"

"Yes, your honor, thank you." She stands up. "The plaintiff wants you to believe she is a loving wife who should be granted a divorce, half of my client's assets along with full custody of their children when I have proof she has also been unfaithful."

"That's a lie!" the wife shouts. "Why are you lying?"

"Order! Order! Mr. Whitlock, I suggest you control your client's outburst before we have a huge problem."

"My apologies, your honor." He leans over to whisper in her ear.

"Ms. Abernathy, continue."

"My client doesn't have an issue with divorcing his wife, his main issue is giving her half of everything he has worked so hard for, as well as giving up his children. He is not perfect but neither is she. We will show the court that my client deserves the right to raise his children without the outrageous amount of money the plaintiff is requesting."

As she finishes her opening statement, the courtroom door opens and in walk my parents. My dad gives me a thumbs up before taking a seat on the back row.

"Very Well, Mr. Whitlock, call your first witness."

"Your honor, I call to the stand Mrs. Tutwiler."

Rueben swears her in.

"Can you state your name for the record?" her lawyer asks.

"Kandice Tutwiler."

"Mrs. Tutwiler, can you tell the court why you are seeking a divorce from your husband?"

"Because he is an unfaithful bastard who doesn't deserve to have a wife."

"How long have you known your husband to be unfaithful?"

"Um, for about the last three years of our marriage."

"Why did you stay?"

"I chose to stay mainly because of our children and also because I loved him and thought he would change, like he always promises to."

"Then why now?"

"Because he never stops lying. He says he wants our marriage to work and that he isn't being unfaithful anymore but I find that hard to believe when a two-month-old baby shows up on our doorstep six months ago."

"A baby that you found to be your husband's?"

"Yes, and that was the end. I mean, it is one thing to consistently cheat on your wife but then to bring a baby home? That means you didn't use any protection and didn't give a damn about me or the family you supposedly love."

"Have your tried counseling?"

"We've tried counseling, marriage retreats, midnight talk sessions… You name it we've tried it, and each time my husband says he is no longer cheating but we all know it's a lie."

"Do you still love your husband?"

"Yes, I will always love my husband, but I can no longer say I am in love with him. I cannot continue to give him permission to hurt me. I've given him thirteen years of my life, seven as being his wife, and it was only to be his arm piece, his homemaker and mother of his children. I don't believe he's ever truly loved me. So, it's time for me to get my heart back."

"No further questions."

"Ms. Abernathy," I say.

"Thank you, Judge Shannon. Mrs. Tutwiler, have you ever been unfaithful to your husband?"

"No."

"Are you sure?"

"Yes, I would know if I was."

"Your honor, we have evidence that Mrs. Tutwiler has been unfaithful to her husband on numerous occasions."

"That's a bald-face lie!"

Chapter 29

"Objection, we were not made aware of any evidence."

"Ms. Abernathy, what is this evidence you have?" I ask.

"Judge, we have text message transcripts that will clearly show a sexual relationship between Mrs. Tutwiler and a male we've identified," she says, handing me copies.

"Objection overruled, I'll allow it."

"Mrs. Tutwiler, I'll ask you again: have you ever cheated on your husband?"

"And I will tell you again, no."

"You do remember that you're under oath," Ms. Abernathy says walking over to the witness stand to hand Ms. Tutwiler a piece of paper. "Can you verify the phone number that's highlighted?"

"No," Mrs. Tutwiler responds.

"Judge, will you instruct the plaintiff to answer the question?"

"She did Ms. Abernathy. Either ask another one or move on," I instruct.

Getting agitated, Ms. Abernathy says, "Mrs. Tutwiler, do you recognize the phone number on this paper?"

"No."

"Your honor," Ms. Abernathy says before I cut her off.

"Ms. Abernathy, what exactly are you trying to get the plaintiff to answer?"

"Whether or not this is her phone number on that printout."

"Mrs. Tutwiler, is that your phone number?" I ask her.

"No, your honor."

"Are you really going to sit on the stand under oath and tell the court this is not your phone number?"

"Ms. Abernathy, you are crossing the line. Move on," I tell her.

"Ma'am, I don't know these phone numbers," Mrs. Tutwiler answers again.

Ms. Abernathy starts to laugh. "So if I dial the number on here, your phone wouldn't ring?" she asks, pointing to the paper.

"I'm not sure what you aren't understanding, but firstly, my phone is on silent so no, it wouldn't ring, but secondly, this isn't my phone number. I don't know why my husband is trying to attack my character but I have never cheated on him and he knows it. For the record, Ms. Abernathy, my phone number ends in 4774 and this phone number is 7447. Maybe your paralegal typed it in wrong but this isn't me."

Ms. Abernathy walks over to the stand and snatches the paper from Kandice's hand. Looking at it, you can see the veins in her neck beginning to pop out.

"Ms. Abernathy?" I say, when she just stands there starring at the paper. "Do you have another question?"

"Uh, your honor, can we take a recess?"

"Yes. It's noon, we'll break for lunch and resume at 1:30PM. Court adjourned."

I make it back to my chamber shaking my head at Ms. Abernathy. She had her ass handed to her by the plaintiff.

As soon as I remove my robe, there is a knock on the door.

"Daddy, what are you guys doing here? Where's Mom?" I ask as he comes in.

"She's out talking to your secretary and you know we wouldn't miss your first day on the bench. I am so proud of you," he replies hugging me.

"Thank you so much. I was so nervous going out at first but I love it."

"I knew you would. Townsend called and wants to have dinner tonight before we leave. Can you and Thomas join us?"

"Of course."

"Good, I already made reservations at Folk's Folly for 7PM."

"I'll let Thomas know."

"Okay, I'm going to go and rescue your mom and then we are going to get out of here. We have to pack up all the stuff your mom has purchased while we've been here."

"What time is your flight tomorrow?"

"Nine in the morning."

"Thanks for coming, Daddy. I'll see you tonight."

After they leave, I sit at my desk for a minute looking over the financial worksheets and the original request Ms. Abernathy made.

Mrs. Tutwiler has been a stay-at-home mom the majority of their marriage. They have two daughters, thirteen and ten. She's asking for $2,000 per month in alimony and $2,000 in child support, as well as full custody of the children. Looking over his finances and the fact that she hasn't worked in over six years, he should have agreed to it because she may get a lot more than that. He may regret coming to trial.

"Excuse me, Judge Shannon," Judy buzzes.

"Yes ma'am?"

"Do you want anything for lunch?"

"No thanks, Judy. I'm going to lie down for a minute. Please don't let me oversleep."

"All right. If you need me, just buzz."

I look over the husband's financial worksheet again and I'm blown away. This man makes over $25,000 per month as director of finance at a major company, yet he's fighting his wife for the $4,000 she's asking. *Smh!*

I close the files and go lie down on the couch in my office. I'm hoping to get about a thirty-minute nap before court begins. I didn't sleep well last night because I was too excited about today.

"Judge Shannon. Judge Shannon."

"Yes?" I say getting agitated at whoever in the hell is nudging me.

"I apologize for disturbing you but Ms. Abernathy and Mr. Whitlock are requesting to see you."

"What time is it?"

"It's 1:00PM, suga. You didn't get to sleep long. Do you want me to tell them to come back?"

"No, no, it's fine. Give me a few minutes then send them in."

Chapter 30

"What can I do for you both?" I ask the attorneys when they walk in.

"Your honor, my apologies for bothering you but my client would like to accept the original deal that was offered to him," Ms. Abernathy says, taking a seat across from me.

"Is that right? And how does your client feel about that, Mr. Whitlock?"

"She wants more in alimony and child support now. She also wants the house they are currently living in and her car."

"Were these things not in the original request?"

"No, your honor."

"Where are your clients?"

"They're outside," Abernathy answers apprehensively.

"Go get them."

"Ma'am?" she asks.

"Go get your clients," I repeat, getting up from my chair.

When they leave, I put my robe on and sit at the table in my office. After a few minutes there is a tap on the door.

"Come in."

"Your honor, this is Mrs. Tutwiler and—"

"I am familiar with them, no need for introductions. Have a seat."

They all look nervous as they sit down.

"Mr. Tutwiler, it is my understanding you are now interested in the agreement that was offered by your wife a year ago."

"Yes ma'am."

"Why the sudden change of heart now?"

"I just want this over with."

"Or is it because your lawyer screwed up this morning?" I ask, looking at her.

"Uh, yea, that too."

"Mrs. Tutwiler, I understand you have some new negotiations. What are they?" I ask grabbing my pen.

"I want full custody of our girls. He can have weekend visits every other weekend and we can split the holidays. I want him to keep health and life insurance on them with me being partial beneficiary. I want $3,000 in alimony, $3,000 in child support and half of his 401k. I also want my name kept on their college fund accounts, the house and my car."

"Is that it?"

"Isn't that enough?" Mr. Tutwiler says, trying to whisper to his attorney.

"If I were you, I'd keep my mouth closed," I tell him. "This agreement isn't filed yet, sir, because she could be asking for a whole lot more. You should be grateful this is all you have to part with."

"I apologize, your honor."

"Oh, I also want to keep our checking account that the house bills are coming out of."

"Hold up," he says, "there's over $10,000 in that account."

"I know," she replies.

"Any objections, Mr. Tutwiler?"

"No ma'am," he says, looking like he's about to cry.

"Then we have an agreement. I will meet you all back in the courtroom in fifteen minutes."

=======

"All rise, this court is now in session. The honorable Judge Camille Shannon presiding."

"You may be seated," I say taking my own seat. I look around the courtroom and notice Jyema sitting in the back. *This bitch has some nerve.*

"Mr. and Mrs. Tutwiler, do you both approve to the agreement that was reached in my chambers?"

"Yes, your honor," they both say.

"Then the court finds that the divorce shall be granted on the grounds of adultery and that Mrs. Kandice Tutwiler is entitled to a divorce as prayed for in her complaint. It is therefore ordered, adjudged and decreed by this Court that a Decree of Divorce is hereby granted to the plaintiff and the marriage relationship existing between the parties is hereby terminated and held for naught, and both parties are hereby released and discharged from all obligations thereon.

"It is further ordered that the agreement entered into is hereby incorporated into the Court's order and is a part of this Decree of Divorce. Both parties acknowledge under oath that they have voluntarily entered into the agreement and that they have made full disclosure of all assets and liabilities, and that they understand the terms of said agreement.

"It is further ordered that Mrs. Kandice Tutwiler is the residential parent and legal custodian of the minor children and Mr. Larry Tutwiler shall have parenting time with said minor children in accordance with the Court's Standard Parenting Order.

"You are hereby ordered to pay Mrs. Kandice Tutwiler a sum of $3,000 per month in spousal support until she remarries and $3,000 in child support. She shall also retain ownership of the marital home and her car, a 2015 Lexus. She shall also retain the active checking account and all monies it currently holds. She is also hereby awarded half of the 401k that is in the name of Mr. Larry Tutwiler which amounts to $51,257.62.

"Mr. Larry Tutwiler, you are to keep health and life insurance on the minor children until they reach the age of twenty-one and Mrs. Tutwiler shall be a partial beneficiary.

"All debt incurred before today, June 29, 2015, shall be divided among both parties to resolve.

"Are we in agreement?" I ask after reading the divorce decree.

"Yes, your honor."

"Then it is so ordered." I hit the gavel.

"All rise," Rueben says, as I stand to leave the courtroom.

Chapter 31

"Judy, can you get the DA on the phone for me please?"

"Yes ma'am."

By the time I finish hanging up my robe, Judy is buzzing with the DA on the phone.

"Judge Shannon, to what do I owe this honor?"

"Why aren't you doing anything about Jyema James?"

"What do you mean?"

"She was sitting in my courtroom this afternoon. I also know that you were made aware of her showing up when my husband was in the hospital, a clear violation of the protection order."

"Yes, I am aware but—"

"But? There is no but. She has now violated the order twice. Why isn't she in jail?"

"It's complicated, Judge Shannon."

"Complicated? Are you fucking kidding me? It was your idea to get the order of protection and now you won't do anything about it?"

"Please calm down. How long will you be in the office?"

"For about an hour."

"I'm coming to you," he says and hangs up.

"Damn it!" I fume, slamming the phone down.

"Are you ok?" Rueben asks, walking in.

"No."

"Is there anything I can do?"

"There was a young woman sitting in the courtroom today. Dark-skinned, short hair—"

"I saw her. She wasn't hard to spot being she was sitting in the back by herself. Who is she?"

"Her name is Jyema James and I have an order of protection against her."

"Why didn't you tell me beforehand?"

"I don't know. I thought she would have learned her lesson by now. I was just on the phone with the DA who isn't doing his damn job."

"I'm trying," DA Brent Walker says as he arrives.

"I'll leave you two to talk. Call me if you need me," Rueben says, closing my door.

"Did you run all the way here?" I ask sitting at my desk.

"Look Camille, I'm in a hard spot with your case."

"Why is that?"

"She's blackmailing me," he says, sitting across from me.

"Who?"

"Jyema."

"What does she have on you?"

"My affair with Chloe."

I laugh. "So let me get this straight: I can't get protection from a woman who is stalking me because you are afraid your wife may find out about your affair?"

"It's more than that, Camille. It can cost me my job."

"Yea well, this is my life. What am I supposed to do? Just allow her to continue to make it a living hell because she knows you're not going to do anything?"

"I'm trying to figure it out."

"How about you charge her for blackmailing you as well as violating my protection order and send her ass back to jail."

"I can't. She has pictures."

"Am I supposed to care? Tell your damn wife and then she won't have anything over your head."

"And what about my job?"

"Either you do something or I'll go above you."

"Please, just give me some time."

"You have one week," I tell him, walking to the door to open it.

"Hey, are you ok?" Thomas asks standing at the door.

"No, but I will be."

He looks Brent up and down. "You look familiar," he says to him.

"I'm Brent Walker, the district attorney. We've worked together before. It's good to see you again, Thomas."

"You too. Now, you want to tell me why you're upsetting my wife?"

"I'll fill you in. DA Walker was just leaving," I reply.

"Judge Shannon, I will get in touch with you soon."

"What was that about?" Thomas asks, pulling me into him. "I came to see how your first day went and it looks like it wasn't good."

"Jyema showed up."

"Really? And what is the DA doing about it?"

"Nothing. That's what we were arguing about."

"This doesn't make sense. If she is violating the order or protection, she should be arrested."

"We are all in agreement on that," I say as he releases me and I sit on the couch.

"So, why isn't he doing anything?"

I look at him.

"What is it?" he asks.

"She's blackmailing him."

"Jyema is blackmailing the DA? With what?"

"He's having an affair with Chloe."

"Chloe? Your best friend?"

"That would be the one."

"So now Jyema has all the power?"

"It seems that way and this is crazy. How am I supposed to get on with my life with her constantly showing up whenever she wants?"

"We will figure this out but—"

"But? What is there to 'but' about? First we had Chelle and now Jyema." I'm getting upset.

Without saying anything he pulls me up from the couch and into his arms.

"What are you doing?" I ask, looking into his eyes.

Smiling he says, "Changing the subject." He then kisses me.

"That'll do it," I say wiping my mouth.

"I came hoping we could christen your new office but it looks like that's been ruined."

I just look at him.

"Why are you looking like that?" he asks, stepping back from me.

"I'm just... I'm loving this new you," I tell him as I go to lock the door.

When I turn around, he grabs me before leading me over to my desk. He commands me to put my hands on the desk. I smile because I don't know what turned this side of him on but I absolutely love it.

He reaches under my dress and snatches my thong off.

"Oh!" This shit is turning me on more and more.

He pushes my dress up, pulls me a little from the desk and spreads my legs. I turn to look at him but he puts his hand on my back to stop me.

"Don't move."

"What are you doing?" I ask him again.

"Taking charge. Don't move."

Who in the hell is this?

Chapter 32

I hear his pants unzip as I impatiently wait for what he is about to do to me. I can feel the juices between my legs starting to run so I take it upon myself to play in my candy box.

Inserting two fingers into her, I let out a soft moan of pleasure just as Thomas brushes up against me.

I remove my fingers and he begins to rub the head of his rock-hard penis against the opening of my girl.

"You want this dick?" he asks in my ear.

"Yes baby, give it to me."

"Say please."

"Please!" I moan a little bit louder.

He thrusts into me as I grab the edge of the desk and, at the exact time, Judy buzzes, "Judge Shannon, if you don't need me, I'm going to head out."

I reach for the phone and press the button to respond at the same time Thomas hits my spot.

"Oh!" I say releasing the button.

"Judge Shannon, are you ok?" Judy asks.

"Uh, yes Judy I am, um, I'm good. I will see you tomorrow."

"Are you sure?"

"Yes!" That was actually in response to Thomas but she took it too.

"Okay, you have a great night and I'll see you in the morning."

I can't even reply because Thomas is sending an orgasm through me that's making my legs weak.

He grabs one of my legs and raises it up on the desk as he continues to thrust into me.

"Oh God, this feels so good."

He then stops.

"What's wrong?"

"Nothing," he says, stepping out of his shoes and pants.

He grabs me and leads me over to the table in the middle of the room. He lays me on my back and enters me again. He has my legs over his shoulders as he plays my girl like a drum. He's beating her something good and the moans coming from my mouth are making great music.

I pull him down to me, covering his mouth with mine as he continues to give me all of him.

"Ooo," I moan into his mouth. "I'm cumm— Oh my God!"

He pulls back and slows down, going in and out. He then takes my hands and pulls them over my head as his strokes get faster.

"Uh," he grunts, as my breath is now caught in my throat from the feelings running through me. I don't know whether to cry or scream.

Collapsing on top of me, "That was good," he says into my mouth as he inserts his tongue.

When I finally come up for air, I laugh. "Where in the hell have you been the past fifteen years?"

I come out of the bathroom fixing the clothes that I just changed into.

"Babe, Daddy wants us to meet them for dinner tonight because they are leaving in the morning. Are you up to going?"

"Yea, I'm always up for dinner with your parents. And it'll do me good to get out."

"Oh, Mr. Townsend will be there too."

"Cool," he casually responds walking over to kiss me again.

"Don't start!" I say pushing him off. "We have plans so come on Thomas 2.0, let's go."

========

Making it home from dinner, I'm exhausted.

"Dinner was great," Thomas says as he undresses in his closet.

"It was, and I don't mean any harm by saying this but I am kind of glad to see my parents head home. I love them dearly but having them here almost two months has become unbearable."

"They only want the best for you."

"I know but I was starting to feel like a kid again with them being here, watching my every move. Don't get me wrong, I always welcome their unsolicited advice but two months of it was forty-five days more than I bargained for." I toss my dress across the room.

"Are you going to let Townsend call the DA about your case?"

"Not yet. I want to see if he's going to do the right thing before I take it over his head."

"Don't wait too long because you know this Jyema chick is crazy, and if she is bold enough to show up in your courtroom knowing you have an order of protection against her, there's no telling what she will do."

"That's what I am afraid of. Not so much her but what she is capable of doing, again. I told him I'd give him a week. If he hasn't done anything by then, I'll take it from there." I sigh. "I'm going to take a shower."

"Can I join you?"

"Haven't you had enough?" I ask.

"Not yet."

"Shit! I need to look at the medicine you're taking."

"Why, you can't keep up?"

"Who, me? Have I ever backed down from you?"

"It sounds like you're throwing in the towel tonight."

"Whatever!" I say, lobbing a pillow at him and running into the bathroom with him on my heels.

Chapter 33

It has been two days since Thomas and I christened this office and each time I look at the table, I can't help but smile.

"Judge Shannon, here are the case files for the breach of contract case," Judy says walking into my office and interrupting my thoughts.

"Thank you, Judy. This one is still scheduled for tomorrow, right?"

"Yes ma'am. Their defendant's lawyer has asked for two continuances so hopefully tomorrow will be the day."

"Great. Thanks."

"No problem."

I look over the case of Dr. Thaddeus Barnett v. Abundant Medical Supplies. Barnett claims the company sold him medical equipment that was faulty and, according to their contract, he is entitled to a money back guarantee that the company will not give him. The doctor claims a GE LOGIQ E9 ultrasound machine they purchased for $65,000 is defective and, per the contract, AMS is supposed to refund the customer at 100%. Dr. Barnett has since been denied his refund and filed breach of contract.

After an hour of peace, Judy buzzes.

"Yes Judy?"

"There's a Lyn Williams here to see you."

"Send her in."

I get up and walk over to the door.

"Lyn, what are you doing here?" I ask, giving her a hug.

"I just came to see your new office and to ask you a favor."

"A favor? What kind?" I question, pointing for her to sit down.

"I need you to take care of Kelsey should anything happen to me. I don't mean full time because she will still have Paul, but I need you to help him take care of my baby should something happen to me."

"Of course I will, but nothing is going to happen to you."

"You don't know that for sure. I'm sick, remember?"

"I get that you're sick but as long as you take your medicine like you should, you can live a full life."

"I know but it's a struggle most days and I've come to realize that even on your best day, you're sick enough to die. I just need to make sure she will be taken care of."

"Well, what can I do to help?"

"Can you rewind the hands of time to before I met Xavier?"

"I wish I could because there are a lot of things I would change about myself too."

"Yea, well, you don't have HIV. I mean, I wake up day after day wondering why this is happening to me. I know I've made some mistakes but I never would have imagined I'd end up with HIV. My entire life has changed." She gets up from the chair. "Paul and I are divorcing and he won't even talk to me. Kelsey is upset because she doesn't fully understand it all and hell, I can't explain it to her because it's hard for me to grasp."

"Is Kelsey back at school?"

"Yes, I finally talked her into going back. She left two weeks ago. I didn't want her to give up college worrying about me."

"She's only concerned about you, like we all are. You go off by yourself and you won't allow any of us in."

"I'm only trying to wrap my head around this. I have HIV, Cam. Me!" she cries as the tears start flowing. "I never thought it would happen to me. I thought I was being safe but man, was I wrong."

"Stop beating yourself up over this. You can't change it now, but you can live with it and you of all people are strong enough to endure this."

"I don't feel like it. My legs feel like jelly every time I stand and I don't know what else to do."

"Yes you do! You fight. Listen, I can't even begin to imagine what you are going through but you have all of us to love you through it."

"Is love enough?"

"It can be. All you have to do is let us help you."

"You can't do anything for me. This disease is inside of me. There's not anything you or anyone else can do."

I pull her into a hug.

"I'm sorry. I didn't mean to bring all of this to your job. I just needed to talk."

"You don't have to apologize. I am always here for you."

"I know and I love you, always remember that."

"You're talking like you're going somewhere," I frown, looking at her.

"I just want you to know that. We've been through a lot together and you could have turned your back on me but you haven't."

"That's what family do, Lyn. I love you too."

"Now, will you promise to watch after Kelsey?"

"Of course."

"Thanks. I'll let you get back to your day."

"I have time to kill, do you want to do lunch?"

"I can't, I have some things to take care of," she answers, walking over to hug me again.

"Are you sure, you're ok?"

"Yes, I will be."

When she leaves I can't shake the feeling that I have in the pit of my stomach. It feels like she was telling me goodbye.

Chapter 34

"All rise, the honorable Judge Camille Shannon presiding."

"You may be seated."

"Judge, we have the case of Dr. Thaddeus Barnett versus Abundant Medical Supplies, case 1742151."

"Thank you, Rueben. Dr. Barnett, you are here today to recover money for a defective machine you purchased from the defendant for your OB/GYN practice, is that correct?"

"Yes, your honor."

I look over to the defendant and no one is there but the attorney. "Mr. Billsworth, where is your client?"

He begins to stutter. "I'm not sure, your honor."

"Was he aware of the court date today?"

"Yes, your honor, we spoke last night."

"Since he has been properly notified and still decided to miss court today, we will continue with the case."

"But your honor, if it pleases the court, may I ask for another continuance to give my client a chance to defend himself?"

"Mr. Billsworth, looking over the case files I see you've already been given two. If your client couldn't find the time to show up today, to defend himself, I will not waste any more of the court's time. Mr. Ross, are you ready to present evidence that proves your client's case of breach of contract?"

"Yes, your honor."

"Then let's proceed."

"Your honor, my client Dr. Thaddeus Barnett purchased a GE LOGIQ E9 ultrasound machine on January 19, 2015 for the purchase price of $65,000." He hands me a copy of the contract. "The machine was found to be defective after it failed to meet the standards of what AMS stated it could do. We have evidence from an independent company who was asked by Dr. Burnett to look into the machine after it failed to do adequate sonograms."

"Have you provided a copy of that report to the court?"

"Yes, your honor. It's there with the copy of the contract."

"Mr. Billsworth, was your client made aware of this report?"

"Yes, your honor."

"What is their response?"

"They don't dispute the fact that the machine is defective and they tried to replace it for Dr. Barnett."

"Yes your honor, but what Mr. Billsworth is not telling you is that this was a replacement machine for the first machine, and neither one worked. Here is a copy of the paperwork showing that," Mr. Ross replies.

"Mr. Billsworth?" I look at him as he rummages through paper.

"Yes, your honor, that's true, but they were willing to replace that one too."

"Look, I don't know about you, Mr. Billsworth, but after the second time, I would be reluctant to accept anything else from this company too."

"I know, your honor, but my client offered to refund $50,000 but the plaintiff declined."

"That is his right. Why should he lose out on $15,000 for a problem caused by your client? As per the contract, your client's contract, AMS agrees to a money back guarantee within thirty days. Mr. Ross, was this file claimed with AMS within the thirty days?"

"Yes your honor, both times. Here is the initial claim, and then the second claim."

I take a few minutes to look over the paperwork of the claims.

"I've reached my decision. This court finds that Abundant Medical Supplies has indeed breached their contract against Dr. Thaddeus Barnett. I am awarding a judgement against them for the total cost of $65,000 that the plaintiff requested, along with his attorney and court cost. It is also noted that the plaintiff did not ask for any additional punitive or consequential damages. It is so ordered. Court adjourned."

"Well, that was pretty cut and dried," Rueben says as we walk back to my office.

"Yea, that happens when the defendant doesn't show up."

He laughs.

"Thank you Rueben, I guess we are done for today."

"Are you leaving right away?"

"No, I'll be here another hour or so to close out both of these cases so that they can be filed."

"Okay. Buzz and let me know when you're ready and I'll walk you out."

"Thanks."

I work for another hour finishing up the paperwork. I grab my things to leave when Lyn comes across my mind. I dial her cell phone from my desk but she doesn't answer. I leave her a message to call me.

Walking out, I meet Rueben.

"Are you ready to go?" he asks.

"Yes, but if you are still working, I'll be fine to walk out alone."

"No, I'm done. Give me one second to grab my things."

Making it to my car, I say, "Thank you Rueben, you have a great night."

"You too," he says, preparing to walk away. "Oh, are you coming in tomorrow?"

"No, I'll probably work from home seeing that both of the cases have been closed out."

"Cool. If you need me, you know how to reach me."

I quickly get in and lock all the doors. I'm not taking any chances with crazy-ass Jyema still walking around.

Chapter 35

Before heading home, I stop by to get a 'massage'. With everything that has been going on, I need to relax.

"Cam, it's good to see you again. Marcelle is waiting for you so you can head on back. Would you like your usual glass of wine?" the receptionist states when I enter.

"Yes, please."

"I'll have it waiting for you by the time you change."

"Good evening, boo. You need an all-over massage tonight?" Marcelle asks as I walk into her room.

"God, yes!"

She bursts out laughing. "Go ahead and get on the table. Lie on your stomach."

I quickly remove my robe and follow her instructions. By the time I am on the table, she presses play on her iPod and a song begins to play that makes me sit up. I turn back to look at her and she smiles.

"That's Juicy by Pretty Ricky," she tells me.

"Wow, ok," I smile.

"Now, relax and allow me to do my thing."

"Have your way, boo."

She drapes the sheet over my butt down to my feet. As I relax, she takes my head in her hands and begins to massage. As usual, her hands feel so good that it makes me forget everything I am going through.

She moves down my back, taking her time. Rubbing her hands up and down my sides, I can't help but to heat up — all over. A slight moan escapes my lips but she doesn't stop. She continues down to my butt and then my legs.

Running her hands in between my thighs, my breathing picks up. She notices but she doesn't linger there. I'm tempted to rush her but I allow her to take her time. She moves down to my feet. Bending my right leg, she takes my toes into her mouth.

I gasp.

I've done some freaky shit in my life but I've never been into toe sucking, however Marcelle has a way of making me change my mind.

"Oh," I moan as she sucks them one by one.

She releases that foot and takes the other one, repeating the same actions. My hands are gripping at the sheet as I try to control my breathing.

"You ok?" she asks.

"Really?"

She giggles.

"Turn over," she instructs, removing the sheet.

Once I am on my back, she climbs on the table, hovering over me. She places her legs on the outside of me as she slides down. She begins to massage my head. As she reaches my neck, her kneads are followed by kisses. She continues to my chest, taking her time to show love to each one of my nipples.

Her tongue then traces a path down until she reaches my navel, lingering there.

"OOH," I cry out, reaching up to grab the back of her head and she doesn't stop. She moves down and blows on my clit causing my eyes to roll. Getting completely off the bed, I take the opportunity to spread my legs. She runs her hand over my lady before inserting her fingers.

I buck a little as she plays my inside like a piano. Her fingers are replaced by her tongue as I cry out in pleasure.

"Don't stop! Please don't stop."

The orgasm takes me over as my legs shake.

"Damn girl! I feel like I need a cigarette."

"Do you want the full experience tonight or are you satisfied?"

"I thought this was the full experience?"

"No, there's more… if you are into strap-ons."

"Oh no, I'm good. I like the real thing but you've been great as usual."

"Are you sure?"

"Yes, this was exactly what I needed. Thank you. I'll see you next month."

Once she leaves the room, I go into the bathroom and take a quick shower. I love the soap and body butter they have here. I will be sure to purchase some before I leave tonight.

"Cam, how was your massage?" the receptionist asks when I go back up front.

"Wonderful as usual."

"I'm so glad you enjoyed it. Do you want to keep the other appointments you have set?"

"Yes ma'am."

"Great, I have you scheduled. Am I charging the usual on the card on file?"

"Yes, and I want to get some of the massage oil, soap and body butter that Marcelle uses."

"Sure thing. Any particular scent?"

"No, surprise me."

She comes back and hands me a bag with my purchase.

"Thank you. Please text me the receipt and I will see you next month."

I get home to find Thomas asleep on the sofa in the den. I walk over and nudge him. When he doesn't move, I start to walk away but he reaches out and grabs me. Pulling me down onto him, he laughs.

"I should have known you weren't asleep."

"I was but I heard you come in. Damn, you smell good. What is that?"

"It's called Magic Body Butter by The Bubble Bistro. You like it?"

"Hell, yes. I want to lick it off of you."

"Good thing I bought some from the spa."

"What else did you buy?"

"Why don't you come and find out."

"Shit, say no more," he says, pushing me off of him. "Let's go!"

Chapter 36

"Thomas."

"Hmm," he mumbles.

"Someone is ringing the doorbell," I tell him, turning the nightstand light on and looking at the clock that shows 2:38AM.

Who in the hell could it be, at this hour?

Thomas and I both get up. I grab my robe as I follow him to the door. Opening it, we come face to face with officers from the Memphis Police Department.

"Ma'am, I'm so sorry to be disturbing you at this hour. Are you Camille Shannon?"

"Yes. How can I help you?" I ask.

"Ma'am, my name is Detective Charmaine Ruffin with the Memphis Police Department and your name was listed as the point of contact for a Lynesha Williams. Do you know her?"

"Lyn?" I ask, confused and anxious. "She's my best friend. What is this about? Is she ok?"

"Is it all right if we come in?"

"Sure." I step back to let them in. "Now, can you please tell me what this is about?"

"I think it would be best if we sit down."

I lead them into the den area. "What is this about?" I repeat after we are all seated.

"There is no easy way to say this but the body of Ms. Williams was found in a hotel room earlier tonight."

"Wait, what? Her body? No ma'am, you must have the wrong Lynesha Williams," I exclaim, jumping up from my seat.

"Mrs. Shannon—"

"No! It's not her!" I begin to cry. "I just saw her yesterday. You're mistaken."

Thomas grabs me. "Babe, calm down and listen to the detective." He guides me back to the couch. "Detective Ruffin, are you sure it's her?"

"Yes sir. She had identification on her but we will need your wife to give a positive ID. Is this your friend?" she asks, handing me Lyn's driver's license.

"Yes, it's her. What happened to her?" I tearfully ask.

"The preliminary results look as if she committed suicide."

"Oh my God! This doesn't make sense. She wouldn't take her own life."

"Ma'am, I know this is devastating news and I am so sorry for your loss but I need to ask you some questions. When was the last time you talked to her?"

"Yesterday. She came to see me at the courthouse."

"Did she say anything that would lead you to believe she would harm herself?"

"No," but then it hits me. "Oh my God, she was coming to say goodbye," I reply as the tears flow. "I cannot believe this."

"She left this note for you." The detective hands me a plastic bag.

I wipe my eyes as I try to read her last words.

Cam,

If you're reading this, please forgive me. I know this is hard to wrap your head around but don't hate me for choosing my way to leave this world, I couldn't take living anymore. I know you're questioning why I didn't tell you when I came to see you but you would have talked me out of it. Don't blame yourself. I've always loved you and I know you love me, and this is why I had to say goodbye in person one last time. Don't cry for me because I am finally at peace. I know it seems crazy but I just couldn't find the peace in living that I hope I can find in death. I prayed and asked God to forgive me and I believe He has. Please take care of Kelsey. I know she's going to be devastated but tell her I love her more than anything. And Paul, tell him I am sorry for everything.

I left a safety deposit box for you at my bank; you should get all the details in the mail in a day or so. It will have the information you need to take care of all of my affairs. Tell the girls I love them and don't be mad. They may not understand it now but I pray one day each of you will see that I had to do this, for me.

We promised to be friends 'til death do us part, this doesn't change; I simply changed my location. Until we meet again know this is not goodbye, it's just goodnight for now. I love you always.

Lyn

Handing her the note back, I am at a loss for words.

"You can keep it, it's a copy," she says pushing it back towards me. "Mrs. Shannon, do you know why Ms. Williams would commit suicide?"

"She's been struggling with her marriage ending and she recently found out she contracted HIV from a sexual partner."

"Was her marriage failing because of the HIV?"

"No, it was failing way before that, but after her diagnosis she started acting differently."

"How so?"

"She disappeared for a while. She only showed up after my husband was in an accident a few weeks back. She hasn't been the same but I never thought she would do this."

"Do you know why she would leave the suicide note to you and not her husband?"

"I can only think because she and Paul were no longer speaking. He filed for divorce the week after she told him she was HIV positive."

"Is he HIV positive too?"

"No, he's fine but he would no longer speak to her."

"Who is Kelsey that was mentioned in the note?"

"Her daughter. She's away at college."

"Thank you, Mrs. Shannon. You've answered everything for me. Here's my card. Since she named you as her next of kin, you will need to come down to formally identify her."

"When?"

"Tomorrow morning. You can go down to the morgue. Here's the information. Again, you have my condolences on the loss of your friend."

Thomas walks them out as I sit on the couch in disbelief.

"Babe," he says walking back into the room.

"Why didn't she ask me for help?"

Pulling me into him, he wraps me in his arms. "This was her battle to fight and she decided how it would end. She told you not to blame yourself. Don't do it."

"I know but—"

"Just grieve for her. Don't try to figure out the why, just mourn her."

"It hurts so bad. It feels like there's a ton of weight on my chest," I say, trying to catch my breath.

"Breathe, babe. Come on Camille, calm down. Look at me." He takes my face in his hand. "Breathe."

"It. Hurts. So. Bad."

"I know, babe, and it's going to hurt for a long time. She was your sister, a part of you, but you can't make yourself sick."

"She's. Gone."

"I know."

He lays my head down on his leg and rubs my back as I cry for my friend.

Chapter 37

Opening my eyes, I realize I'm still lying on Thomas. Feeling me move, he wakes up.

"Babe."

"I'm going to the bathroom. You can go on back to bed, I'll be right behind you."

"Are you sure?"

"Yea, I won't be long."

We walk down the hall together. He gets into bed and I go to the bathroom, closing the door. Looking in the mirror, my eyes are swollen and bloodshot red.

My tears mix with the cool water I splash on my face. I grab a towel before reaching into the medicine cabinet for a pain pill. I need something to help me sleep for at least a few hours before I have to break the news to Paul and the girls.

I leave the bathroom and make my way back to bed. Sliding under the covers, I allow my sorrow to put me to sleep.

"Hey! Camille, wake up."

I open my eyes to find Thomas sitting beside me.

"What's wrong?"

"Nothing, but it's almost 7:30 and the kids are up. We have to break the news to them before they leave for school. And there are some phone calls you need to make."

I sigh.

"I know it's not going to be easy but I am right here with you."

"I know. Give me a few minutes, ok?"

"Sure."

After taking a little time to get myself together, I walk into the den where Thomas has called Courtney and TJ.

"What's going on?" Courtney asks.

Since it's taking me a minute to answer, Thomas interjects, "Your mom and I received some bad news earlier this morning about your Aunt Lyn."

"What kind of bad news?" she questions looking from Thomas to me. "Mom? What kind of bad news?"

"She's, um, she's gone baby. She died yesterday."

"I don't believe that. I just heard from her yesterday morning."

"You did?"

"Yes. She sent me a text saying she wanted me to know she will always love me. What happened?"

When neither of us replies, she stands up.

"What happened to her?"

"They think she committed suicide."

"Why?" she cries. "Why would she do that? She said she loved me, she wouldn't leave us like that."

"She had her reasons, baby. We may not understand them now but it was her choice," Thomas replies.

TJ hasn't said a word.

"TJ, are you ok?" I ask.

"Why does bad stuff keep happening to us?" he yells. "First, you are on the news, then Dad's accident and now Auntie Lyn is dead. It's not fair!"

He runs out of the room.

"TJ, wait."

"I'll go talk to him," Thomas says.

"Courtney, baby, are you ok?"

"What about Kelsey? Have you talked to her?"

"Not yet. I am about to call them now. I wanted to tell you all first."

"How?" Courtney asks as tears fill her eyes.

"How what?"

"How did she die?"

"We can discuss it later. Right now, I need you to be strong for Kelsey because she's going to need us."

"I'll be in my room," she says leaving the den.

Thomas still hasn't returned from TJ's room so I decide to make the necessary phone calls. I have no idea what I will say but I can't prolong it anymore.

Paul is the first call and it's the hardest thing I've ever had to repeat, and I still have to do it a few more times.

It seems like my heart breaks a little more with every call. By the time I finish the last one, all of the girls have made plans to meet here at 9AM to accompany me to the morgue.

"You ok?" Thomas asks when he walks in and sees my head in my hands.

"When it seems like things are finally starting to go right, we get hit with something else."

"We will get through it. God will give us the strength, and I know He will because I've asked. We have to believe that."

"I do believe that, but seeing the hurt in the kids and then hearing the girls cry out in pain is just too much."

"It may seem that way but you're Lyn's next of kin so even though it may not seem feasible now, you've got to remain strong."

"How am I supposed to do that when it feels like my legs won't move? All I want to do is crawl under the covers in our bed and cry myself to sleep."

"That would be the easiest thing to do but you know you can't do that."

"I know. But in a few hours, I have to identify the body of my best friend."

"After that you have to plan her funeral and then you'll have to pick out the clothes she'll be buried in and where she will be buried. So, even though you want to crumble right now, you can't. What can I do to help?"

"You can start by telling me that everything will be ok?"

"Everything will be ok, eventually. What else?"

"A hug."

"I can do that."

"Thank you for being here. I know we've had a rough year but I cannot imagine my life without you."

"I wouldn't be anywhere else."

Chapter 38

"Are you Camille Shannon?" this lady asks when we walk into the medical examiner's office.

"Yes."

Extending her hand, she says, "My name is Kathy Dwyer, I'm a grief counselor with the ME's office. I will be here to help you through this difficult time."

"Thank you, Ms. Dwyer. This is Ray, Shelby, Chloe and Kerri. Lyn is... I'm sorry, Lyn was our best friend," I say through my tears.

She hands me some Kleenex and says, "I know this is hard but please don't hesitate to ask me any questions you can think of. Right this way."

She leads us into a small conference room. It isn't cold and grey like I'm used to seeing on television; instead it's warm and comforting.

"Please have a seat and call me Kathy. As I stated, I am a grief counselor and I will walk you through the identification of your loved one. I will be here through the entire process so if there are any questions, ask them. There are no wrong or right ones."

"Will we be able to see her?" Shelby asks as she holds Chloe's hand.

"No ma'am. You will identify her through a picture. This will be difficult but—"

"Can we get on with it?" I ask abruptly. "My apologies for interrupting you but I need to get this over with."

"Yes ma'am, I understand. I'm going to give you a picture of your loved one on this clipboard. You can take all the time you need to flip it over." She slides the clipboard towards me. "The picture is only of her face and it was taken by the medical examiner. Again, take all the time you need."

As Ray grips my left hand, I take a deep breath with my eyes closed. I wait for what seems like forever because I'm not ready to see her face. I finally release Ray's hand and flip the clipboard over.

"Oh!" I cry out, placing one hand over the picture and the other over my heart which feels like it's shattering into a thousand pieces. The room fills with pain as the other girls cry out in sadness.

I finally pass the picture to the other girls. My tears momentarily cease but not the indescribable pain I feel at this very moment.

"Why would she do this?" Chloe sobs as Shelby consoles her. "She had to know this would hurt us."

"She wasn't thinking about us," Kerri angrily says. "She was being selfish."

"Stop it!" I yell. "Just stop. We don't know what she was dealing with because we never took the time to ask her. We were the ones who were selfish."

"I know this is probably one of the hardest things to do and being angry is part of the grief process, but don't allow it to consume you. Don't let the anger you are feeling overshadow the fact that you've lost someone important. Whatever your friend was dealing with, please understand, suicide to the person who commits it isn't selfish: to them it is the only way out. You cannot blame yourself and don't blame them. The best way to deal with this is to simply grieve; that's it. Don't try to understand or even question it, just grieve," Kathy shares.

"I'm sorry, Cam, I just don't understand why she wouldn't confide in us," Kerri weeps.

I get up to hug her. "None of us understand but it was her choice. We also have to understand that we were not in her shoes."

"Kathy, can you tell us how she actually died?" Ray asks.

"Not at this moment. The ME will finish the autopsy and the results will be available in a few weeks."

"Did she suffer?" I ask.

"I'm sorry but I cannot give you the answer to that. What I can do is give you some resources to help with your grief. I am not going to lie, it's going to be hard. Losing someone is hard but an unexpected death is one of the hardest pills to swallow so it's going to take some time to deal with. Don't allow anyone to stop you from grieving and please don't make any rushed decisions right now. Give yourself time to deal with the loss you all just suffered. You will be angry, but deal with it by helping one another. You'll want to question why but there is no right answer that anyone can give you to make it better. Allow your good memories to help you now. Don't dwell on the why because you may never know. I can tell by all gathered here that she was indeed loved. Focus on that."

"When will her body be released?"

"The autopsy should be complete within two days. We will then release her body to whatever funeral home you choose to use."

"Thank you, Kathy."

"No thanks needed. Camille, I do have some paperwork for you to fill out."

"Sure.

"Is there anything else I can do for the rest of you?"

"No but thank you for everything," Ray answers.

"Here's my card as well as some information on grief counseling. If there is anything you can think of or if I can be any assistance, do not hesitate to call."

"I will meet you all out front," I tell the girls.

Once I complete all the paperwork, we all walk out clinging to one another. Getting settled into the car, I let the girls know about the letter Lyn left.

"What did it say?"

"You can read it when we make it back to the house."

"Have you talked to Paul?" Shelby asks.

"Yes, this morning before I called you all. He's supposed to call once he makes it back from picking up Kelsey. I asked if he wanted to come with us but he declined."

"Man! I never thought we'd be here at this point in our life," Ray says as she stares at the building.

"None of us did."

Chapter 39

Lyn's Celebration of Life

As we gather outside to enter the church, my legs feel like they'll give out at any moment.

"You can do this," Thomas says, squeezing my hand.

"I don't know if I can, it's too much."

He removes my shades and wipes the tears streaming down my face.

"I'm right here," he says. "I'll help you."

We're standing behind Paul, Kelsey and Lyn's mom and dad. Paul hadn't shed one tear, not even at the wake as Kelsey screamed and cried for her mom. I don't know if his anger was getting the best of him or if he was merely being strong for their daughter. He has refused to talk to me about Lyn and he didn't want anything to do with planning her service. I didn't push him on it but it didn't stop me from planning a celebration I knew she would love.

My kids are behind me with my parents who flew in for the service, and the girls and their families are behind them.

As the funeral director ushers us into the church, my stomach is in knots. This is the last time I will see the face of my best friend, my sister, and it's taking everything in me not to turn and run. Thomas is holding my hand but it seems like everything is moving in slow motion.

There are flowers everywhere and a picture of Lyn sits next to her casket. It was taken during our last vacation to Mexico and in it she is smiling as if she's the happiest person on earth. *Boy, how life changes.*

Kelsey and Paul are first at her casket and, just like the night before, Kelsey breaks completely down. Hearing her cries fill the church is too much for Paul, who finally breaks. His brother eventually gets him to leave the casket as he leads him to his seat on the front row.

Lyn's mother and father are next and her mom's sobs are as equally heartbreaking.

By the time I make it to see her, I am numb. I place my hand on her chest as the other girls step up to join me. They each place their hand on mine as I silently pray and we weep. I pray her dying was not in vain and that she has finally found the peace she so desperately sought.

"We will miss you, Lyn. I will miss you. Rest in sweet peace, baby girl." I turn and grab Thomas' hand before walking to our seat. Each of the girls linger there saying their own goodbyes before taking their seats.

Kelsey has to be taken out as they prepare to close the casket because she can't take it. I cannot bring myself to watch it either because it makes everything so real.

The program begins and it flows beautifully. Kelsey is escorted back in by her dad but she keeps her head buried in his chest the entire time.

Finally it is my turn to speak. I ask God to strengthen me as I stand to walk up to the podium.

"Wow," I say clearing my throat. "Looking at each of you gathered here, I know Lyn was indeed loved. This is by far one of the hardest things I've ever had to do but I could not allow some generic words of gratitude to convey my thanks to each of you who have called, came by, sent flowers, dropped off food or simply said a prayer for us. You all will never know how much it means. I never thought I would be saying goodbye to my sister this early but—"

I take a second before I continue. "Depression is real, y'all. Please don't allow anyone to tell you it isn't. If you or a family member is suffering with it, don't suffer in silence; ask for or seek help. Don't think you will be judged by those who love you because you won't. Get help. Do not suffer by yourself and please don't feel like suicide or hurting yourself is the only way to cope. Depression is a silent disease that affects a lot of people. Just because you think someone may have it all together, they can be drinking tears for water behind closed doors. Don't take a second of your life for granted. If one somebody can be saved through us losing our sister then her dying was not in vain. Again, I thank each of you. When you return to your normal activities, when you can see your loved one face to face, don't take them for granted. And please don't stop praying for us."

I walk pass her casket and place my hand on top of it before taking my seat.

The service continues and Pastor Ansley begins the eulogy.

"Brothers and sisters, we didn't come here today to mourn the death of our sister Lynesha Williams but we come here to celebrate her living. The Bible says in 1 Thessalonians 4:13-14, 'And now, dear brothers and sisters, we want you to know what will happen to the believers who have died so you will not grieve like people who have no hope. For since we believe that Jesus died and was raised to life again, we also believe that when Jesus returns, God will bring back with him the believers who have died.' Yes, I know death has snuck up on you snatching breath from your lungs, beats from your heart, steps from your walk and has even caused tears to fall, but in order to be present with the Lord on the other side, we have to die on this side. Oh, I know it doesn't feel good but it has to happen."

He continues and before I know it, the service ends. We make our way back to the cars as we stop to hug people offering their condolences. I've never understood why people say, "I'm sorry for your loss." What are they sorry for? Are they sorry to see us in pain? Are they sorry she killed herself? What exactly are they sorry for?

Chapter 40

The ride to the cemetery is extremely quiet. We all make it to the burial site and I sit with a purple flower in my hand. It was Lyn's favorite color. I'm grateful to the florist for getting them for me on such short notice but I had to have them. I try to listen to Pastor Ansley but my mind is filled with so many other thoughts. I am so angry at Lyn for leaving us.

Shelby nudges me to let me know it's time for us to place our flowers on her casket. As we stand, Pastor recites John 14:27-28, "Peace I leave with you; my peace I give you. I do not give to you as the world gives. Do not let your hearts be troubled and do not be afraid. You heard me say, 'I am going away and I am coming back to you.' If you loved me, you would be glad that I am going to the Father, for the Father is greater than I."

He instructs us to place our flowers as he delivers the burial prayer.

"Forasmuch as it hath pleased Almighty God of his great mercy to take unto himself the soul of our dear sister here departed, we therefore commit her body to the ground; earth to earth, ashes to ashes, dust to dust; in sure and certain hope of the Resurrection to eternal life, through our Lord Jesus Christ; who shall change our vile body, that it may be like unto his glorious body, according to the mighty working, whereby he is able to subdue all things to himself. Amen."

He then turns the service back over to the members of the funeral home. "This now concludes the burial of our dear sister Lynesha Williams. We thank you for taking the time to share with the family today and we ask your continued prayers for them in the days, weeks, months, and years to come. You may now return to your cars."

I stop by her casket one last time before returning to the car.

"Are you going to the repast?" Ray asks.

"No, I'm going to pass. I'm tired and I just can't take the hugging, the condolences and the looks of pity anymore."

"I understand."

"Thanks. Can you please let Kelsey know I will call to check on her later?"

"I will. Call me later," she says hugging me.

I find Thomas and let him know I'm ready to go. Courtney is riding with Kelsey and TJ is with Shelby.

=======

Making it home, I go straight to the bedroom and kick off my shoes. Getting into bed, I grab the note Lyn left from my nightstand and begin to read it, again.

"Why did you have to leave?" I whisper.

Gripping her final words to my chest, I release the tears of anger I feel at this very moment. Yes, I am mad at Lyn. I know it was her decision but it makes me mad just to think about Kelsey and how she's suffering. I'm trying to understand and I don't mean to be angry.

"Babe, are you ok?" Thomas asks, coming into the room.

"Why did she do this?" I ask, wiping my face with my hand.

"Why are you torturing yourself?"

"I'm just so mad at her."

"You have a right to be but you're going to have to let her rest in peace. It's the only way you will be able to get over losing her."

"I know but I cannot get Kelsey's screams out of my head. I cannot forget how she pleaded with her mom to come back."

He climbs into the bed and pulls me into him as I release my tears of prayer. "Why couldn't I help her?"

"She didn't want your help. She felt like this was her only way. Didn't you look at her?"

"Yes."

"And didn't you see how peaceful she looked?"

"Yes."

"You've got to know that she's at peace now and there is nothing anybody can do to bring her back."

"I know but—"

"No buts, Camille. You will have to grieve your best friend but don't keep doing this to yourself. You have to let her go, not forget her, but let her rest in peace so that that you can find peace. Stop questioning why it happened when she's already told you why. Now, you need to sleep," he says sliding from the bed. "Do you want me to call Dr. Scott and see if she can prescribe you something?"

"No, I'll lie down, I promise, but before I do, can we talk for a minute?"

"Can't it wait until after your nap? You haven't slept in days."

"No, I need to say this before I lose my nerve. Please, it won't take long."

Chapter 41

Sitting completely up, I take a breath to calm the butterflies in my stomach.

"What is it, Camille?"

"You know that we've had a rough year. With everything we've been through then with your accident and now Lyn's death, it seems like my life is in a whirlwind and I can't get out. I can't live like this anymore, Thomas."

"You aren't thinking about hurting yourself, are you?"

"God, no! It's just that," I pause, "I've been keeping something from you and it has almost cost me everything. I am tired of hiding behind it."

"Just tell me."

"You've been telling me that I need to get my shit together before I end up with no one in my corner, and after Lyn I can't imagine needing you and you not being there. I don't want to lose you. Please tell me you won't leave me."

"I am right here fighting with you. However, in order for us to win we've got to be on the same page. I know what I want, do you?"

"I do now. I realize that I've made a mess of my life, can you please forgive me?"

"What am I forgiving you for?"

"For not being what you needed. For pushing you into the arms of another woman because of what you were missing from me."

"Where is all this coming from?"

"Seeing my best friend in that casket has made me grateful for everything I have but in order for me to really appreciate the place I'm in, I have to deal with where I came from. That starts with telling you the truth."

"Ok," he slowly responds.

"When we met, I was in a dark place. I didn't care about people's feelings because I'd put up a wall to ensure I wouldn't be hurt, by anyone, again."

"Hurt? You thought I would hurt you?"

"Just hear me out. I didn't know what your intentions were in the beginning. You were just another man who talked a good game. But then you wouldn't leave me alone. You wouldn't take no for an answer. Even though I had a wall up and put on a façade, it only covered the pain and shame that was inside of me, and you stayed. Then you made me a wife and mother and I've become good at maintaining this smokescreen but it's slowing killing who I am supposed to be. I get up in the morning put on my makeup, comb my hair, slip into my fancy suits with my five-inch heels and a smile and I pretend, never actually seeing what it is costing me."

"What are you getting at?"

"You remember when I had the four-hour session with Dr. Scott?"

"Yea," he slowly replies.

"Well, I finally admitted something to her that I had never shared with anyone before that, including my parents. When I was in my second year of law school, I was raped by my advisor."

"Raped! Why didn't you tell me?"

"Until then, I was ashamed that I allowed someone to hurt me so I shut it out. By the time you came into my life, I was at a point of 'hurt them before they hurt you'. I was lost and the only way I dealt with it was sex. You have to understand, I wanted to forget what happened to me because it was the most degrading thing I've ever had to endure and sex, for me, was… is what I used to numb the pain. I was so messed up on the inside that I didn't even realize I was that person who didn't care who she hurt. Being hurt at the hands of someone I trusted turned me into this person I hate. But I thought as long as I wasn't physically hurting anyone, I could continue living this way but I don't want to be this person anymore, Thomas. Will you please forgive me?" I cried.

"Wow. I… I don't know what to say."

"Say you'll forgive me."

"Why didn't you think you could trust me enough to tell me then?"

"I didn't know how. I've being walking around a shell of a person to simply survive."

"But why now?"

"Because whether I wanted to believe it or not, I was once walking in the same shoes as Lyn. I was once the person who thought suicide was the only way out. The only difference between me and Lyn, I didn't go through with it."

"What stopped you?"

"You did. When we met you were so persistent. You wouldn't allow me to sit in my apartment and just study and you loved me despite me pushing you away. You loved my broken pieces even if they cut you from time to time."

"Again I have to ask, why are you sharing this now?"

"I have to in order to get past all of this crap that is in my head. It feels like I am going crazy and I am tired. Tired of hurting and I am tired of hurting my family. I don't want to become the person who feels trapped and sees suicide as the only way out. I'm asking for help because I know now that I need it. I need help!"

He doesn't say anything. He gets up and walks out the room. I bury my head in my hands as I cry. I am not crying because I'm sorry for finally telling him, I'm crying for the release.

"I will help you as long as you are willing to help yourself because I will not fight for you if you aren't willing to fight," he states coming back into the room.

"I am willing."

"Then I can't ask for anything else. Time will tell if you are serious. Now, try to sleep. We can talk more when you get up."

========

I wake up to find Thomas asleep beside me. I look over at the clock and it reads 3AM. *Damn.*

I realize I am still dressed from the funeral. I quietly slide out of bed and walk into the bathroom. I peer in the mirror and I look a mess. I turn the water on in the shower as I undress. I step in and allow the hot water to run down over me. For the first time in a long time, I feel free.

After drying myself and oiling my body. I slip into my nightgown. I slide under the covers next to Thomas and he stirs a little as I get close to him.

I lie there for a few minutes unable to go back to sleep. I look over and Thomas is on his back so I move my hand down his chest until it reaches the top of his boxers. I quickly slide my hand into them and begin rubbing on his semi-erect penis. He moves a little but it doesn't stop me from sliding underneath the covers. I remove it from his boxers and suck it into my mouth.

Taking all of him in, I suck a little harder coming back up before removing him and doing it again.

"Hmm," he moans. "What are you doing?"

I don't say a word. I use my tongue to massage his balls while using my hand to make sure he gets as hard as I need him. The tip of my tongue finds the tip of his penis and I work like they've missed each other for years.

Thomas' hand moves to the back of my head as I continue to suck and lick him.

Taking his balls into my mouth he moans his approval for me to continue.

I release him and move up to ride my stress away. I mount him, taking him inch by inch.

"Ah," I groan once he is fully inside of me. I lean over and kiss him as he opens his eyes. I smile at him as my pace increases.

He doesn't say anything as he grabs my waist and I sit up. He grabs my breast and I place my hands on his chest.

"Oh, you feel so good," I say into his ear.

He flips me over, placing my legs over his shoulders as he re-enters me.

"Don't stop," I cry out in pleasure.

He places his hand on the headboard and pumps into me like he has a score to settle.

"I'm coming, don't stop," I tell him while spreading my legs to intensify the feeling. "Shit!"

As my orgasm peaks, he lies on top of me, slowing his pace.

"Wrap your legs around me," he breathes in my ear.

"Uh, ah," he grunts before rolling off of me. "What a way to wake up."

Chapter 42

It's been a month since Lyn was buried. I've been working longer hours getting prepared for the next session of court cases. Since my confession session with Thomas, things have been better. He is finally back to work, which is a good thing.

I haven't heard a peep from Jyema and that scares the hell out of me. I've called to speak to the DA but he hasn't returned any of my calls so I decide to pop up at his office.

"May I help you?" his receptionist asks.

"Yes, I need to see DA Walker."

"Do you have an appointment?"

"No, but tell him it's Judge Camille Shannon."

She buzzes him before turning back to me. "Judge Shannon, he said he's going to be tied up for a while but he'll call you when he's done."

"I'll wait." I take a seat.

After a thirty-minute wait, his office door finally opens and out walks Brent with Jyema behind him.

"You have got to be kidding me," I exclaim, standing up.

When he sees me, he looks like a deer caught in the middle of a highway.

"Judge Shannon, it's great to see you again," Jyema smiles.

I look at Brent. "Camille, I thought you'd left," he says.

"You thought wrong."

"Shit!" he says, rubbing his head.

"Yea, you fucked up. Especially since you just finished screwing the person you're supposed to be prosecuting."

"I'm not f—"

"Dude, stop! Zip your pants."

Jyema giggles while walking out then she turns back and says, "Same time next week, right?"

"Jyema, just go!" he growls.

"I've seen all I need to see." I turn to leave.

"Please Camille, don't leave. Come in and let's talk."

"No thank you. But I think filing a claim of misconduct on you is my next step. I've given you ample time to handle this but instead, you sleep with her?"

"Can you give me five minutes to explain?"

"I'll give you three," I say stepping into his office. "Go."

"I'm sorry. Please don't file a complaint on me."

"Are you serious? This crazy motherfucker is still walking around free and instead of you doing your job, you're having sex with her."

"I didn't have a choice."

"There's two choices Brent, right or wrong, but we both know which one you made and now I've made mine."

"Please, don't do this. I'm trying to figure out how to fix this."

"And when are you doing that, in between orgasms?"

"You don't understand. This can cost me my job and my marriage."

"What can cost you your marriage?" his wife, Monica, says walking in. "Are you two having an affair? I should have known. Damn it, I should have known you would sleep with her."

"Pump your brakes, sister. I'm not the one sleeping with your husband but he's going to wish I was when I am done with him."

"Brent, what is she talking about?" Monica asks.

"I'll explain it to you tonight. Right now, I really need to talk to Camille alone."

"I'm not going anywhere until you tell me what the fuck can cost you your marriage."

"He's sleeping with Jyema."

"Jyema? Why does that name sound familiar?" she frowns.

"She the woman he's supposed to be prosecuting for stalking me."

"Baby, it's not what you think. She's blackmailing me," Brent says.

"Blackmailing you with what?"

"I've been having an affair—"

"I know."

"Wait, you know?" He looks stunned. "How did you know?"

"You don't think I can tell? Your entire demeanor has changed."

"Damn, this shit keeps getting worse," he whines.

"No, you made it worse because had you confessed to me, you probably wouldn't be in this mess."

"But she threatened to send pictures to you and the media."

"So, we could have dealt with that," she shrugs. "Had you been thinking with your brain instead of your dick, you wouldn't be standing her now looking foolish."

"This shit can cost me my job."

"Fuck your job!" she screams.

"It looks like Jyema has made a fool of you. I'll be in touch," I say leaving them alone.

I walk out of his office and immediately call Mr. Thompson. I let him know I need that favor after all to handle this mess with the DA and Jyema. I have no doubt he will get it taken care of.

Chapter 43

Before heading home, I stop by Dr. Scott's office.

"Camille, did we have an appointment?" she asks when I catch her getting ready to leave.

"No, and I apologize for showing up without calling."

"Is everything ok? Come on in."

"I told Thomas."

"That's great. How did he take it?"

"He took it better than I expected. I thought he would be furious with me but he wasn't. He been so caring and understanding."

"Why did you think he would be upset?"

"Because I never told him but it has been a huge relief to get it off my chest."

"What made you tell him now?"

"Losing my best friend. I realized while making her funeral arrangements that it could have been me."

"Have you been suicidal?"

"Not recently, but I've been in that dark place before. I understand how your life can change in the blink of an eye from one bad decision. That was me. I've been at a point where I thought taking my life was the only choice I had left, but then I met Thomas and he loved me through it. That's why I was so angry with Lyn because she could have talked to me and I would have loved her through it."

"Suicide is a subject a lot of people doesn't want to talk about. For one, they don't think it can happen to them and, when it does, they aren't looking for help: they are looking for a way out."

"But she had choices. She didn't have to do this."

"Do you remember how you were when we started almost two years ago?"

"Yea."

"And do you know how hard it was, for me, to break down the wall you had up?"

"I get it Dr. Scott, but what does that have to do with what Lyn did?"

"You chose to get help; she didn't. Lyn probably felt like she had come to the end of her race and she had no more strength to run. It was her choice. It doesn't negate the fact that you were friends and you loved her. I am sure she loved you too, but that couldn't stop the pain she felt or the plan she made."

"I understand that now but it's still a hard pill to swallow."

"Death is never easy, but what are you going to do to ensure Camille doesn't go back to that place?"

"I'm letting everything that doesn't mean me any good go. I'm tired. I'm tired of wearing a mask, I'm tired of being someone that I'm not and I am tired of running."

"What's different now?"

"I almost lost my husband who stormed out after an argument with me. Then I still have this case with Jyema hanging over my head and it almost cost me my life and my career. Then, if things couldn't get worse, my best friend dies. So, Dr. Scott, everything is different."

"I hear you Camille, but why did it take all of this to get you to see the tornado you were in the middle of? It touched down a long time ago. Why are you just now seeking help?"

"I guess you can say I was like the people who try to ride out the storm. They think it'll never happen to them until it's too late and you realize you're trapped with no way out. I was trapped in pain and bitterness from what happened to me in my past and I didn't grasp that until I couldn't find my way out. It took me watching my life almost get blown away before the cold reality slapped me in the face."

"The sad reality is that it takes getting pushed down to your lowest point before you realize there's a way out. And it's been there the entire time."

"You're right, but going down surely makes me appreciate being up."

"Well, I am glad we've finally had this breakthrough. Are you done with the extramarital affairs?"

"Yes. I promised Thomas that I was going to do better and I meant it."

"You promised Thomas, but what about making a vow to yourself?"

"I have."

"You don't sound convincing."

"Really? You don't feel like you got your money worth unless we argue, do you?" I laugh.

"I'm not trying to argue with you tonight because I am glad I finally get to break through your barriers. Let's leave it at that."

"Thank you. Now, I'm not going to keep you anymore tonight. I'll see you in two weeks."

"I look forward to it."

Chapter 44

I swear Dr. Scott can ruin a wet dream. I did make a promise to Thomas but one more for the road won't hurt. *Will it?*

"Hey, you still up?" I ask when he answers the phone.

"Yes. What's up?"

"Can I get a quickie?"

"Where are you?"

"Outside."

He walks out and my mouth is watering. I pop the locks on the doors as I motion for him to join me in the back seat.

He stops and waves for me to let the window down. "Camille, what—"

"Just get in," I say cutting him off.

He quickly opens the door and slides in. I can tell by his facial expression he is at a loss for words.

"What are you up to?"

"Don't talk."

I reach for his crotch and trace his manhood with my fingers. *Thank God he has on basketball shorts.* I quickly take off his shirt and slide down to remove his erect penis from his shorts. My eyes are on his as I lick my lips preparing to taste him. I take him into my mouth savoring the taste while slowly taking inch by inch.

"Damn girl!" He moans as I widen my mouth to take all of him, tightening my muscles with each suck.

"Um, yea, make it sloppy for Daddy," he says, grabbing the back of my head.

I give him the side eye. His talk has been unusually dirty lately. "How do you want it, Daddy?" I ask sarcastically while looking into his eyes.

His eyes widen when he realizes what he's said.

"Relax and tell me. How do you want it?" I ask, while sucking on the head.

"Just like that, ugh, like that! Shit!"

"Like this, Daddy?" I say sucking him harder and making sure to get it very wet and sloppy. I let my saliva slide down the side as my hand gets faster and faster with the rubbing.

He has both hands on my head as I make sure he is hitting the back of my throat.

"Wait," he says. "You're going to make me nut if you keep that up. Let me feel you."

I remove my panties and sit backwards on his lap. Sliding him into my wet and throbbing candy box, I grab the back of the seat as I position myself to ride. He has one hand on my waist and the other playing with my nipple.

"Hmm, you feel good."

"Do I?"

"Yes, damn good."

"Show me, make me cum."

I guess he's up for the challenge because he grabs me around the waist with both hands and begins pounding into me. I lean back into him as he moans into my ear. I match his pumps by grinding into him as I feel my orgasm forming.

"Don't stop."

I pull my legs up so they are now on each side of him as I play with my clit. "Open your eyes," I tell him.

I want him to see me squirt. *This is a pleasure he's never experienced with me.*

"Um, I'm about to cum and I want you to watch."

I rub my clit harder as the sensation builds. "Oooo! Shit!" I scream as I squirt all over the back of my seats.

"Damn girl, what in the hell was that? That shit was sexy as hell!" He turns me over with his pace intensifying and I lose my breath. I have to put my hands on the car door to keep from hitting my head.

"You've been holding back on me."

He finally releases into me and kisses me. "I want to see that again."

"Okay."

"Tonight."

I laugh.

"I'm not kidding so bring that ass on in the house," he says, putting his shirt back on.

"Okay, I'm coming." I press the garage door opener. "I'll be right in, Mr. Shannon."

Epilogue

A year later

"Hey babe, you ready to go? Church starts in forty-five minutes."

"Yea, I'll be right out. Let me finish this email to Dr. Scott."

Dr. Scott,

I received your email and everything is great on my end. I know it's been a while since I've been in for a session but I've been so busy with work. Yes, I am still enjoying life with my family and friends and I couldn't ask for it to be any better.

I know working with me was probably one of the most challenging things you've done but you stuck with me and for that I am appreciative. I told you, after our last session a year ago, that I was determined not to go back to the place I was in and I've held true to that.

And because of that my life is… It's great! I am the happiest I've ever been and I didn't think it was possible. The kids are doing great. Courtney is 16 and a junior in high school. TJ is 14 and growing like a weed. They are away visiting my parents at the moment and we are enjoying the peace. As for me and Thomas, our relationship is stronger and I cannot believe I was risking it all over wanting something that I already had at home.

Oh, we finally dealt with his accident about six months ago. He has been so guilty over Chelle's death that it was starting to weigh heavily on him. We met her mom and dad and they don't blame Thomas. Apparently Chelle had done the fake pregnancy thing before but they thought she was done with mess like that. They learned the hard way that she wasn't.

I am just glad Thomas was honest enough with me about his feelings so that we could deal with it together.

Yes, I am still grieving the loss of my best friend Lyn. Although she lives on through her daughter Kelsey, who I get to see often, the hurt of her not being here is still present every day. Xavier, the bastard who gave Lyn HIV, was finally prosecuted and sent to prison. I made sure to be at every one of his court appearances along with his baby momma. She wanted to ensure he wouldn't get off. Praise God!

As for Lyn's store, a couple of days before her funeral, I received a packet in the mail that included her insurance policies — one for me and one for Kelsey — the deed to her store and the keys to her car and condo. It took me three months to clean out the condo but I eventually did it. I still haven't been to her gravesite but her birthday is coming up so we will see.

Yes, I am still on the bench. I am going into my second year as Judge Camille Shannon and it has been amazing. There's a lot of work but it's so worth it. Almost losing it last year put a lot of things in perspective for me and burying that drama has been a burden lifted from my shoulders.

Jyema was finally sent to prison because this crazy heifer was relentless. She would show up at my house and job like she ran the world because she thought she'd never be prosecuted but DA Walker eventually confessed to everything. It did cost him his job but he was able to save his marriage. I guess that can be considered a half win, right? Plus, his wife was into girls after all and she had a thing for Chloe too. (She'll probably be your next client, LOL.)

The other girls are doing great. Shelby and Derrick are expecting their third child. Ray is still Ray even though she and Anthony have decided to get married. Kerri and Mike are still good and she just opened her third location for the bakery. Chloe's marriage went up in smoke when Brent's story hit the TV but she is enjoying life. I am keeping an eye on her because I don't want her to go down the same path I did.

Anyway, thank you for everything, Dr. Scott. You helped me make amends with the demons of my past and for that I am extremely grateful. Cam has been retired and she only comes out on rare occasions for my husband. Scout's honor.

I do struggle sometime, I won't lie, but I've learned to be honest with Thomas and he appeases me by going to a swinger's club but the only thing we bring home with us is a smile.

I know I'm rambling and Thomas is calling my name so I'll let you go. Thanks again for being there for me through these last two and a half years. It was rough starting out but I don't regret my struggle at all. It made my book so much more thrilling.

Who knows, maybe you will hear from me again.

Until then,

Cam!

Again, I thank you for taking the time to read my work! I cannot express what it means to me every time you support me!

Be on the lookout for the next series … Chloe's Sidechick Tale! Coming 2016

For upcoming contests and give-a-ways, I invite you to like my page: Facebook.com/AuthorLakisha or follow my blog authorlakishajohnson.com or you can email me at authorlakisha@gmail.com.

If this is your first time reading my work, please slide over to Amazon and check out the other books available:

A Secret Worth Keeping

A Secret Worth Keeping: Deleted Scenes

A Secret Worth Keeping 2

Ms. Nice Nasty

Ms. Nice Nasty: Cam's Confession

Sorority Ties

And my two **Devotional Books**:

Doses of Devotion

You Only Live Once

Now Available - Ms. Nice Nasty

Camille Holden-Shannon has always been who she
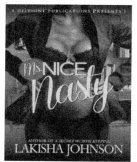 says she is, a woman who can
command a courtroom and
bedroom without opening her
mouth! She's sexy, confident and
not afraid; her credentials speak
for themselves. She loves her
family and her career but she
cannot deny the fact that she
loves sex and lots of it. She doesn't break up homes;
she simply gets what she needs and she's gone!

Her career suddenly takes a turn in the right
direction and she is thrown into the public's eye and
all hell breaks loose! A secret adds more fuel to the
fire already burning inside her chaotic home and to
make matters worse she finds herself being
tormented by a ghost from her past! Can she hold it
all together or will she break under the pressure?
Will Ms. Nice Nasty hang up her stilettos or can she
come out on top like she's known to do.

Now Available - *Ms. Nice Nasty: Cam's Confession*

She thought revenge was the answer...

For Camille, she proudly proclaims to be "unapologetically Cam" but now that her life is in a downward spiral with no way to escape, will she see the error of her ways?

For months her therapist has been trying to break down her wall and when Camille tearfully admits the ultimate betrayal, from her past, she now has to face the cold reality staring her in the face.

Yes, she thought getting revenge would satisfy the fire burning in her soul but it only added fuel. Now, her life burning out of control and she has to decide whether to fan the flames or put it out in order to save her marriage and career.

What will she do? Find out in this special edition of Ms. Nice Nasty. Also, get a sneak peek into Ms. Nice Nasty 2 with a look into the first two unedited chapters.

CPSIA information can be obtained at www.ICGtesting.com
Printed in the USA
BVOW06s1116220816

459715BV00048B/169/P